MERLIN PROTHEROE, PRIVATE INVESTIGATOR

Twenty Short Stories featuring the Penarth Detective

by Rob Falconer

Rob Falconer was born in Cardiff, the capital of Wales, far too long ago for him to remember the actual date. Having gained a degree in psychology from Cardiff University, he joined the family coach business "for a while" (actually around nine years). A history of the company can be found on his website, www.robertfalconer.co.uk.

He later became a computer programmer, before he and his job parted company in 2001. He has since written a number of short stories, and won competitions with The Times, International Mensa (he is a member), and the South Wales Echo. He has had a number of poems published in various anthologies :

'Puzzling Poems to Drive You Crazy' (Oxford University Press, edited by Susie Gibbs)
'How to Survive School' (MacMillan, edited by David Harmer)
'Read Me Out Loud!' (Pan MacMillan, edited by Gaby Morgan)

He has also written for comedy shows on both BBC and ITV.

His first book, 'The Return of Inspector Pirat: His First Book' (yes, I know, but you'll understand when you've read the book), came about because he often couldn't sleep, and amused himself by thinking up puzzles, which he then put into print. So, blame insomnia. Many of the stories are based around locations he has visited, such as a gîte in the Loire, on which 'Truck Stop' is based (he has difficulty in sleeping abroad too).

His second book, 'Pirat's Early Cases' was published in paperback and Kindle versions in late April 2016.

Nine more Inspector Pirat books were published between February 2017 and August 2023 (full details are at the back of this book).

A sampler of four Inspector Pirat stories, 'A Taste of Inspector Pirat,' is available free on Smashwords.

As there seemed much local interest in the long-established coach company he and his family operated from Llanishen, a northern suburb of Cardiff, from 1919 to 1982, he published a personal history of the company in February 2018, 'Memoirs of a Coach-Operating Man' (paperback and Kindle versions are available on Amazon).

Three other books, unrelated to either Inspector Pirat / Pratt or the family coach company, are

'A Little Bit of Immortality' (about one man's quest to live forever)
'A Brief History of Time Travel' (a fictional collection of short stories about the pioneers of time travel)
and
'Joan Malone Alone' (written for younger readers)

all of which are available on Amazon.

'How to Retire Ungracefully' (a short book - or a long pamphlet - about how to enjoy retirement, and definitely not to be taken seriously) is available free from Smashwords.

His interests include pétanque, the cinema (but not necessarily modern cinema), crosswords and problem-solving, history, and reading detective fiction. His favourite detective author is Edmund Crispin, some of whose puzzles are truly ingenious, but laced with plenty of (often literary) humour.

He lives in Llandough, in Penarth, South Wales.

First published (Paperback / Kindle):
February 2024

Edition 1 – February 2024

ISBN (paperback): 9798877390973

Copyright Rob Falconer

Rob Falconer has asserted his right under the Copyright, Designs and Patents Act 1988 to be the identified as the author of this work

All rights reserved

**Visit Rob's website:
www.robertfalconer.co.uk/**

For Dawn, for her help and advice

Index

Preface

Starting Up

Case 2023/001 – The Maltese Raven

Case 2023/002 – Seeing the Bigger Picture

Case 2023/003 – Farewell Party

Case 2023/004 – Behind the Times

Case 2023/005 – Pier Pressure

Case 2023/006 – Hair Apparent

Case 2023/007 – Is This a Dagger?

Case 2023/008 – I Spy

Case 2023/009 – On the Scent

Case 2023/010 – Too Much Caffeine is Bad for You

Back to the Drawing Board – a diversion

Case 2023/011 – The Woman Who Loved Fatty Arbuckle

Case 2023/012 – The Route of All Evil

Case 2023/013 – Following Up a Lead

Case 2023/014 – Honeymoon Sweet

Case 2023/015 – If You Go Down to the Woods Today …

Case 2023/016 – Post Bellum

Case 2023 /017 – How Long Would it Take the Police to Find Dead Bodies if it Weren't for Early-morning Dog Walkers?

Case 2023/018 – Up Before the Beak

Case 2023/019 – A True Gentleman

Case 2023/020 – Below Cheese Copse

Preface

After eleven books of detective short stories featuring Inspector John Pratt and his alter ego, Juan Pirat, it seemed time for a change.

One publisher suggested that I should write about a detective who worked in a real location, rather than the fictitious Alefordshire, perhaps somewhere local, somewhere I knew well.

So, this book is about a private investigator, Merlin Protheroe, his sister, Guinevere, and his brother, Arthur, who is in the regular police force.

And the setting is Penarth, where I live.

It is a small seaside town which once, with nearby Cardiff, shared in the boom-time profits of the coal export industry, but which is now a sleepy seaside resort with a pier and some nice small shops, but, as of 2023, no longer any banks.

I would like to thank Joe Heller of Wisconsin for his caricature of me. Do I really look like Cary Grant?

And I would particularly like to thank Dawn F. Taylor, not only for her nitpicking proofreading, but also for her very valuable comments and input. I'm still waiting for her book to be written and published.

Again, I would like to thank all my readers, including family and friends, for their support over the years. I certainly wouldn't have had the nerve to continue without you!

Rob Falconer
Llandough, Penarth
February 2024

Starting Up

"Have you heard of the Postcode Lottery?" asked Guinevere Potts, clearly elated.

"Never a good thing, Gwen," replied Merlin Protheroe, her brother. "It means, for instance, some areas get better health facilities than others."

"No, Merlin, you don't understand. I've *won* the Postcode Lottery. It's not the National Lottery, so it's not ten million pounds or so, but it's quite a lot." She seemed a little reluctant to say exactly, or even roughly, how much.

"I'm very happy for you," beamed her brother. "Will you spend it on a cruise around the Mediterranean, or a trip to see your relations in Australia, or an extension to your extension?"

"Well, my husband earns enough for everything we want, and there's nothing I do want anyway. And I wouldn't even consider the options you've suggested. I get seasick. I hate my relatives in Australia because they always phone us up before six in the morning, and anyway I loathe those Christmas cards they send us showing girls in bikinis lazing on sun-kissed beaches. And we still haven't found enough stuff to fill the last extension we had."

"No, what I want to do is something I know you've wanted ever since you got sacked …"

"Made redundant," corrected Merlin.

"… And that's to start a detective agency."

"Oh, I know it'll initially only be divorce cases and shadowing shady husbands, but it'll be fun, and we might get some real cases eventually."

Merlin wondered how long 'eventually' would be. Or even when they'd be lucky enough to have their first divorce case.

And he certainly wasn't sufficiently well-built to handle any 'rough stuff.' He was 55 years old, five-foot-eight, of slim build, with prematurely white hair. He often seemed thoughtful and distant, which is why, coupled with his almost-mystic Christian name, he was often referred to as 'The Wizard' … although perhaps not often enough for his liking. He was therefore considering growing a long white flowing beard, as well as enormous bushy white eyebrows, but his sister insisted on trimming these frequently, usually, he said, when he wasn't looking …

As a youngster, he was usually to be found with his nose in a book about crime and detection. So, at the same time as his brother, Arthur, he had applied to join the local police force, but had been unsuccessful, he surmised because his approach was too theoretical and cryptic. However, his brother had been accepted, Merlin assumed because he was down-to-earth and just plain unimaginative. So Merlin had got a job in telecommunications, until both the word and the staff levels were truncated. He had since been trying to find something worthwhile to do with his life. He had tried bowls (but he kept on getting his whites grass-stained), French boules (he gave up as he couldn't pronounce 'pétanque'), fishing (the only thing caught was Merlin, when he was overcharged for his rod) ... And he had finished with U3A, the University of the Third Age, when he discovered he wouldn't be able to actually get a degree with them.

As a contrast, his sister *was* rather well-built, taller than Merlin, and very good at extracting information and gossip from people. She was 48 and worked part-time as a receptionist in a local dental surgery, but she was also an occasional reporter on the Penarth Equitable, a politically biased local free newspaper, the free often stretching to its payments to reporters. But she only reported facts and left the lies to the editor.

"And, anyway, there's also Arthur," Guinevere continued. "As he's in the local police force, perhaps you could even help him out sometimes. He might need to call on you for advice."

Merlin nodded. He was sure it was more likely to be the other way around.

But he agreed, trying to appear to be at least a little reluctant …

-oOo-

Merlin and his sister had often commented on the large swathes of local shops closing down or being opened as charity shops, coffee shops and fast-food emporia ... although, it has to be said, mainly charity shops.

Not that many of the local inhabitants needed charity in the Protheroes' home-town of Penarth in South Wales. It was a fairly well-to-do area where most of the complaints to the council were about dog mess on the streets. There was a Victorian arcade in the centre of town, similar to the famous ones in Cardiff city centre, and a pebbly beach by the promenade, together with a Victorian pier. Merlin often thought that not a lot had happened there since the demise of Queen Victoria.

So they had hoped to secure a first-floor office at a knock-down price right in the town centre, perhaps overlooking the roundabout near where most of the banks had once been. However, although shops were closing down, it seemed that offices were in much greater demand, and they realised they would be forced to pay a rent far higher than they had expected.

The estate agent suggested a "much sought-after bijou office suite in a central location."

"It's overlooking Belle Vue Park," he said. Belle Vue Park was well away from the centre of town, but a pleasant enough location.

However, although the building may have been overlooking Belle Vue Park, the office certainly wasn't, as it turned out to be a room at the rear of the first floor overlooking a back lane. As the man from the estate agency said, it was "quite a nice back lane."

Even if the room was very small, they decided they would take it, at least until their reputation and, of course, finances increased sufficiently to enable them to move into somewhere more impressive.

Inside they installed a desk from IKEA, to which they moved Merlin's home computer. A corded phone would suffice for the time being, they decided. There was just enough space for a small desk for Guinevere, as Merlin's personal secretary and confidante. And she would certainly have to be his confidante in such a small office, unless she waited outside in the corridor whenever clients discussed their more intimate problems with Merlin.

With no space for a wardrobe, they had to make do with an umbrella stand and a hat stand. There were only three chairs, so, if more than one client visited, they might have to make the client stand too.

Finally, an artist friend was asked to write Merlin's name and occupation on the glass panel in the door, as this was what Merlin remembered from just about every film noir he had ever seen. Merlin had wanted Consulting Detective, and Guinevere had wanted either Private Eye or Private Dick, but they finally settled on the more prosaic:

Merlin Protheroe
Private Investigater

It seemed as if the artist friend might have been suffering from delirium tremens, but only slightly. Either way it only cost Merlin £10, which the artist said he would be happy to accept as a cheque made out to Bargain Booze.

Luckily, Guinevere was able to scratch out the centre of the second 'e' in "Investigater," to make it look a little more like an 'o.'

A few flyers were printed out on their old HP printer and distributed selectively to homes where they knew there to be some domestic disharmony or to small firms with cash-flow problems. They also put an advert in the local free newspaper, although they were shocked to find that the advertising wasn't free.

It was decided that Merlin would investigate cases involving adultery and Guinevere would handle debt collection. Well, she had the build for it.

And finally, they decided to number their office 221B.

-oOo-

But both of them were surprised how quickly they had their first case.

Case 2023/001
The Maltese Raven

It was Thursday.

Merlin Protheroe leant back in his office chair, the black luxurious one with the wings and high back which he'd managed to pick up cheaply from an online website. He watched the rain run down his office window.

He was idly wondering when his first case would turn up when he sensed that someone female was approaching his office. Her perfume entered the door thirty seconds before she did.

He swivelled gently around in his chair to greet his visitor.

Had he been Sam Spade, he would have described her as one of the classiest dames he'd ever set eyes on.

He immediately christened her Miss Wonderley.

She was dressed in a wet PVC hat and an even wetter duffel coat. From under her hat, long dark hair cascaded to her shoulders. Perhaps she had a hair problem. Piercing blue eyes stared out from a stunningly beautiful face. Above her wide, sensuous mouth, a surprisingly snub nose completed the picture. It needed wiping.

Even her duffel coat couldn't disguise the full figure underneath. A man could get all steamed up thinking about it. She looked like a sexy Paddington Bear.

"Can I help you?" Merlin asked.

"Are you Merlin Protheroe?"

"I am. What can I do for you?"

He gently tipped his chair back. He always believed in relaxing with a client.

"Are you OK?" Miss Wonderley asked, as he struggled off the floor and set his chair upright again.

Merlin nodded.

"Shall we start with your name?" he suggested.

"I'm Sheila Hammett, but most people call me Raven."

She tossed her dark hair back as if she were appearing in a shampoo advertisement on television.

"You're not from around here?" asked Merlin, detecting an accent.

"Well, I was born in Malta, where I met my husband, who was with a Welsh stag party. Anyway, my husband is the reason why I'm hiring you. He's vanished. His name's Gareth Hammett."

"Gareth left our house this morning at about nine, but he never got to work. He always arrives at nine thirty, but I just phoned his office and they said they hadn't seen him at all this morning. Obviously, I can't go to the police as it's too early, but I am so worried about him."

As it was now only nine forty, the police certainly wouldn't have been interested yet … and indeed not for some time.

Merlin nodded again. "I can certainly start searching for him. Has he any distinguishing features?"

"Well, he only has one leg after an accident with a bus."

"Which one?" asked Merlin.

"The number 92 from Penarth."

Merlin noted that down.

"And your address and details?" he asked, as he moved the blotting-paper away from the corner of the desk where water was dripping off her hat.

She gave her address, and then added "39-24 …"

Merlin realised he might have other things on his mind after he interrupted her with, "Not your vital statistics, Madam, just your phone number please."

She looked taken aback, "Oh, but I *was* giving you my telephone number …"

She also gave Merlin details of her husband's Volvo.

Merlin got out a map of Penarth to check on the address. It was a small town, but he loved it. It was *his* town. Full of expensive houses on one side, and mean, squalid areas with seemingly endless back alleys on the other. Rich people, poor people, happy people, frightened people. The town seemed full of people of every race and creed, of every vice and every pleasure. It wasn't a beautiful town, but it was his town. He loved it.

"You've got the map upside-down," Miss Wonderley pointed out.

Merlin put down the map in a crumpled heap. He never had been any good at refolding the things.

"I think I can sort this out, Madam. I just need to show you details of our charges and for you to sign this document."

"Oh anything, but please be quick."

She signed and left in a cloud of French perfume.

Guinevere had been listening all the while.

"Well, I certainly can't afford that sort of perfume. I have to buy Rive Droite or Chanel number 4 from the man in the pound shop. How are you going to approach the case?"

"Let me think for a while, Gwen."

The case all seemed rather strange. Why had Miss Wonderley been so quick to assume that her husband had gone missing? Why had she phoned his office at nine thirty to check whether he'd arrived? And Merlin had himself phoned the office to confirm that she had made that phone call. She'd arrived at Merlin's office so soon after nine thirty, she must have phoned from just outside. And why was she in such a hurry? Why had she not considered that his car might have broken down or been involved in some sort of accident, perhaps not with the 92 bus this time?

Merlin began to suspect what might have happened.

"Well, I think I ought to have a word with the Plassey Street Regulars," he muttered.

Thinking of the Sherlock Holmes stories, Guinevere asked, "Don't you mean Irregulars?"

"No, they all enjoy a pretty good diet," Merlin replied, putting on his trench coat and venturing off in search of the small army of itinerant kids he'd recruited for his underworld investigations.

-oOo-

Later that afternoon, Kevin Rice mounted the stairs to Merlin's office and opened the door without knocking. He stood there twisting a cloth cap in his hands. His clothes were quite threadbare, but he was able to show Merlin a photograph of a Volvo on his brand new iPhone.

"Whereabouts?" asked Merlin.

"In the public car park down by Tesco," replied Kevin. Merlin knew the one he meant. Kevin handed over a well-presented bill for his services.

Merlin paid up and then contacted his brother, Arthur, who was a proper policeman. He was sure there was something here that might interest him.

-oOo-

Later that afternoon, Merlin phoned Miss Wonderley and arranged for her to call back to the office. He said her husband's car had been located, and that she should settle her bill in cash before he would divulge its whereabouts.

She arrived almost immediately and paid the bill.

"Let's start from the beginning, Mrs. Hammett," said Merlin, only just stopping himself from addressing her as Miss Wonderley.

"You husband should have left your house at nine this morning. But he didn't … or rather, not of his own volition. Admittedly, he was in the car, but he wasn't driving. He was in the boot. You had intended staging some sort of accident, perhaps a crash and then a fire, to cover up the fact that you had just murdered him."

Mrs. Hammett stuttered something and then sat down heavily in the spare chair, which she had originally declined.

"But someone …. and we still don't know who … fancied your Volvo more than you did your husband. They stole your car whilst you were locking up the house. But they dumped it the minute they checked in the boot. And we have now managed to locate the car."

"Where?" queried Miss Hammett, her eyes ablaze.

"Oh, it's too late now. The police have been called and are examining the contents. I'm sure they'll find plenty of evidence."

Miss Wonderley beat a hasty retreat whilst Merlin put the cash in his petty cash box.

It was still Thursday.

The rain was still running down the window.

Penarth was a mean town.

Case 2023/002

Seeing the Bigger Picture

Merlin Protheroe and his sister Guinevere had been called out to the grandly styled John Dunstable Art Gallery and Museum in the countryside in the Vale of Glamorgan. It was, in fact, merely an average-sized house in small and unimpressive grounds.

"It's not an art gallery really," said the butler, Mann, who greeted them at the door. "My master painted an awful lot of pictures and liked the sound of their being displayed in an art gallery."

"Or perhaps I should have said he painted a lot of awful pictures," he added mischievously.

Merlin was quite surprised at this show of levity, as the master of the house, John Dunstable, had recently been stabbed to death in the main gallery.

His wife, Matilda Dunstable, at least was rather more sorrowful. She frequently abused her handkerchief with rather stentorious noises.

"I found your number in the phone book and I thought I'd ask you for help. To tell you the truth, I'm not at all satisfied with the way the police are handling this. They seem very, shall we say, flat-footed. To them, it just seems to be another murder …" She shrugged rather resignedly.

"And who was the police officer in charge of the case?" asked Merlin, hoping that it might be his brother Arthur Protheroe. That might make investigating the case much simpler.

"Oh, some idiot called Detective Inspector Henry Medlar," Mrs. Dunstable replied, to Merlin's disappointment.

Mrs. Dunstable led them into the main room, until recently a hive of activity with a doctor and a few members of the forensics department busying themselves around the body. It was now empty of life and even John Dunstable had moved on, albeit not under his own steam.

"I found my husband lying back in his chair, a letter-opener in his chest." Merlin could never understand why people chose to have such a lethal weapon lying innocently around, purely to avoid the ignominy of having raggedly opened envelopes.

Merlin asked, "Has anything been taken? Is anything missing?"

Mrs. Dunstable had clearly already been asked that question. "Well, I have had a good look around this room, and there is absolutely nothing of any importance missing. And whoever was visiting my husband certainly didn't venture into any other room, as it's only a small house and I would have known. And I am afraid I have no idea who he or she was."

"In fact, there is only one item I cannot find."

She pointed towards the wall away from the large windows that looked out onto the front lawn. A series of paintings, about thirty of them in an almost circular arrangement, nearly filled the entire wall. But there was one area of the wallpaper, quite a large patch in the very centre, that was faded, suggesting that a picture that had once hung there had been removed.

"Do you know which painting was hung there?" asked Merlin.

"Oh yes," replied Mrs. Dunstable. "John always liked to show friends and visitors around his paintings, while I listened, or, after a while, pretended to. It was quite a large painting, which he called 'A Glamorganshire Idyll.' I am afraid I don't think his paintings were very good, but he enjoyed painting them. He also bought an occasional painting, but he didn't have the money to create a collection that would really be sufficient to justify calling this an art gallery."

Merlin had no eye for a good painting, but he certainly didn't feel many, if any, of the paintings on display were any good, and certainly not of any real value.

He wondered why anybody would kill somebody to steal a worthless painting … or was it worthless?

"Do you have a picture of or perhaps a copy of the painting?" asked Merlin.

"My husband always kept all his works catalogued meticulously. I have the book here."

A large and sumptuously bound portfolio was lying prominently on the desk.

Merlin donned his gloves and opened the book to the page indicated by Mrs. Dunstable.

The painting was dire.

"This was my husband's favourite painting, probably only because it was his largest canvas."

Merlin could imagine the disgruntled butler suggesting that, as a canvas, it would probably be better put to use as a tent.

Merlin looked up at the wall.

"All the paintings seem to be laid out almost symmetrically," he said.

"Oh yes, my husband liked to paint, as it were, to order. When he was planning the 'Art Wall,' as he called it, he made a number of paintings in particular sizes just to even it all up symmetrically, to balance it all out, as it were."

"Have you got a picture of the 'Art Wall' as it originally was that I can borrow?" Merlin asked.

"I can do better than that. For when visitors called, and only once in the proverbial blue moon that would be, my husband had a number of professional photographs taken of the whole wall, so he could sell them to people. I think he actually sold one. But you can have a copy, gratis, of course. And here's one of 'A Glamorganshire Idyll.'"

Merlin thanked her and looked at the proffered photograph of the 'Art Wall.' It all seemed hopelessly and clinically symmetrical. The paintings formed a large, almost perfect circle on the wall. It was as if the size and orientation of the paintings were far more important than the subject or the quality of the picture. He took a photograph with his mobile phone of the 'Art Wall' as it now was.

"Did your husband have any enemies?" Merlin asked … although it was obvious that he had at least one.

"Nobody at all, really. Hardly anyone ever visited, and certainly nobody revisited, in case they were shown around the paintings all over again."

"In fact, the only visitors in the last few months were a crew from BBC Wales, well, I say crew, but it was only Harold Dempster and one cameraman. They were filming for an episode of 'For Art's Sake.' It was only a week or so ago, so it hasn't been broadcast yet. But you can discount Harold Dempster OBE, as he insists on styling himself, as the thief, as he is renowned for his taste in art and his collection is fabulous ... far better than all this junk. If anybody stole that painting, it had to be someone with no artistic taste whatsoever ... perhaps the cameraman."

Merlin made a few notes and resolved to check whether the cameraman, presumably not being an art aficionado, might have made a repeat visit.

-oOo-

But the cameraman, Jerry Thomas, had a perfect alibi ... and anyway he seemed to have almost as much knowledge about art as Harold Dempster OBE.

-oOo-

Merlin sat back in his chair and looked at his photograph of the 'Art Wall' and the professional diorama that Mrs. Dunstable had given him. There was something rather disturbing about the display, even apart from the obsessional symmetry.

He tossed a picture of 'A Glamorganshire Idyll' over to Guinevere.

"What do you think of that, Gwen?" he asked.

Guinevere screwed up her eyes. "It's hideous," she averred.

And Guinevere, Merlin reasoned, knew nothing about art. There again, he knew plenty of people who probably couldn't even spell 'art' without some deep thought.

Merlin nodded, as if he had expected that response. He started comparing the photographs again. Only the one painting seemed to disturb this wall of symmetry.

Merlin thought for a while.

"I'm popping down to Jenkins," he said.

Harry Jenkins was a photographer friend of Merlin's. He managed to get an image of one of the paintings enlarged.

Merlin then sought out Digby Simpson. He knew a bit about art.

"Are you sure that's one of John Dunstable's?" he asked incredulously when shown the blown-up photograph. "But his paintings are junk, and this one's rather nice. It almost looks like one of J.M.W. Cunningham's. He had a brilliant future, but he was killed in the trenches in the First World War. Not a lot of his stuff survives. I bet this isn't really by him, though …"

"Can you recommend any local art expert who might be able to confirm who the artist is?" asked Merlin.

"Well, you could try Harold Dempster OBE, although he may be a Sir by now. He's well-known. He does a lot of stuff for the BBC. Or there's Derek Hellaby."

Merlin thanked him and made an appointment.

-oOo-

Derek Hellaby lived in a small house in what used to be where students lived in the Cardiff suburb of Cathays, before most of them (or at least those sponsored by foreign governments and rich companies) migrated to the many high-rise blocks of student accommodation scattered around the centre of Cardiff. Every available inch of wall space was taken up by paintings, in many different styles and all infinitely superior to the work of John Dunstable.

"Can you tell me about this painting?" asked Merlin.

Hellaby looked at it, got rather excited, but then calmed down a little.

"This is a joke, eh? A copy by someone … er, someone very talented? You must give me his name."

"What can you tell me about the painting?" insisted Merlin.

"Well, I have no idea who painted it, but it's a remarkable copy of the style of J.M.W. Cunningham,

a very talented painter who died in the First World War. Have you got the original?"

Merlin shook his head, but admitted he thought he knew where it might be.

-oOo-

Merlin was beginning to get an idea who his killer might be. He managed to check on his alibi, which was non-existent.

Merlin decided it was time to contact his brother, Detective Inspector Arthur Protheroe.

He told him what he reasoned had happened and who the killer must be. He suggested checking the CCTV cameras along the route to the art gallery at the relevant time, looking for a specific car.

Merlin was sure that there would be DNA evidence on one of the paintings from the 'Art Wall' that would be conclusive.

-oOo-

Merlin made an appointment to meet Harold Dempster OBE at his sumptuous penthouse overlooking what had once been Cardiff Docks but was now the up-market Cardiff Bay.

"So, where is this painting by J.M.W. Cunningham?" he asked.

Dempster shook his head as if to suggest that he had no idea what Merlin was talking about, but his reaction confirmed Merlin's theories.

"I can assure you I would absolutely love to have anything by Cunningham. Alas ..." He spread his fingers resignedly.

"Look," explained Merlin, "I've examined the pictures of John Dunstable's 'Art Wall' and it's obvious that the large painting known as 'A Glamorganshire Idyll' was moved from the centre to the edge of the display, replacing a much smaller painting, thus upsetting the balance of the display. And that's not the way that John Dunstable would have arranged things."

"Whatever painting occupied that position on the edge of the display was the one that was stolen. And I have proof that it was one that was painted by J.M.W. Cunningham."

Merlin omitted to mention that it might only have been an excellent copy ... or that any proof he had was rather tenuous.

Dempster just stared at him.

Merlin nodded resignedly. "A police officer will be here at any moment to arrest you. They have proof from CCTV cameras that your car was on the roads nearby, and that your car actually turned into the driveway of the art gallery a few minutes prior to John Dunstable's murder."

"I also gather than you have no alibi for the period in question."

"Furthermore, they have recovered fingerprint evidence left by whoever moved 'A Glamorganshire Idyll' from the centre of the display to the edge. I think you know where we'll find a match for that."

Suddenly there was a knock at the door.

Dempster blanched.

As Dempster seemed to have no inclination to do so, Merlin got up and let Detective Inspectors Henry Medlar and Arthur Protheroe in.

-oOo-

Indeed it was confirmed that Harold Dempster OBE had no alibi for the time of John Dunstable's death; that the fingerprints collected from 'A Glamorganshire Idyll' matched his; and that a genuine painting by J.M.W. Cunningham that was lying hidden in his penthouse flat matched the picture that had been on John Dunstable's wall.

Merlin sat back in his chair in his office. He just hoped his brother would get some kind of credit for his work on the case.

He summed the case up for Guinevere's benefit, "Dempster must have seen the painting when he visited Dunstable for the BBC programme, then went back later to try and buy it, no doubt for a ridiculously low figure, and then attacked poor Dunstable in a blind rage when his offer was turned down. He stole the small painting by J.M.W. Cunningham, which had been on the perimeter of the display, and moved 'A Glamorganshire Idyll' from the centre to take its place, in order to suggest that only the worthless piece of art had been taken."

"After all, nobody would ever suspect an art expert of stealing 'A Glamorganshire Idyll.'"

Merlin relaxed, pleased at his success on the case …

… and at the nice cheque from Mrs. Dunstable.

Case 2023/003

Farewell Party

All Saints Parish Hall, adjoining All Saints Church in Victoria Square in Penarth, is a rather splendid old building designed by John Coates Carter, who designed many buildings in South Wales. It is a fine example of the Arts and Crafts Movement.

Alongside is the Lesser Hall, built in 1964, and today a farewell party for Dorothy Snyder was being held there. Dorothy herself had checked that the hall was sufficiently clean and well-presented and had ensured that the event would be well-attended by letting it be known that there would be plenty of Bollinger flowing and that the catering would be in the hands of a very prestigious London firm, Hallett and Dubois. She had realised that, with her reputation in the office, she would need a lavish inducement for her colleagues to attend.

For, in fact, nobody liked Snidey, as she was known. Dorothy herself could easily understand why and didn't relish the idea of sitting alone in the hall drinking bottle after bottle of expensive Champagne … for a number of reasons.

So she had lavished a lot of money ensuring that everyone would want to attend the party … even if they left immediately after eating.

Which is why Dorothy had ordered the caterers to arrive quite late, after the cutting of the cake and her speech.

And indeed they arrived at the same time as Detective Inspector Arthur Protheroe. He had been driving his brother Merlin back from a visit to a local restaurant when the message had come through to divert to All Saints Lesser Hall, so Merlin had tagged along.

Snidey had been found stabbed to death in the hall toilets.

-oOo-

Everyone looked a little confused and embarrassed, but also rather worried.

DI Protheroe talked in a general way to everyone, and soon gathered how hated Snidey was. And it seemed that she had been very selective in choosing who to invite to the party. Her boss, Harry Andrews, was there, as well as quite a few of her office colleagues, but also Dwayne Crump, the office work experience boy, and Molly Porter, the tea lady (who was proud to boast that she also did coffee too). No-one seemed to know why these last two had been invited, as Snidey was particularly rude and arrogant towards both of them, probably because they were so much lower in the office hierarchy than she was.

Miss Snyder had been stabbed in the ladies' toilet using the knife that would have been used to cut the cake. The knife had been left in place. The Forensics team leader was quickly able to announce that there were probably no usable fingerprints on the knife, so it must have been wiped clean, or the killer had worn gloves, or both.

Miss Snyder had specified what should be on the cake, having ordered it from a local bakery, rather than from the caterers, and so she had it all ready in the hall kitchen. She had gone into the kitchen with Molly Porter to collect the cake.

The cake itself was a little odd. The icing consisted of a 3D model of the office Miss Snyder worked in, complete with representations of the twelve guests at the party. Miss Snyder had told Molly Porter she intended to cut the cake in front of her guests, dissecting each figure with her knife. But first she decided she needed to visit the toilets before her speech and so had left the kitchen.

Whilst the doctor and Forensics completed their investigations, DI Protheroe continued chatting with those in the hall. He was just about to start more formal individual interviews when, suddenly, Merlin called him from the kitchen. DI Protheroe considered just ignoring him, but Merlin had a strangely urgent tone in his voice.

"OK, what is it?" asked DI Protheroe resignedly. He was already anticipating a banal comment and feared the worst when he saw an iPad in Merlin's hand. Having searched the internet for a tablet for himself only recently, DI Protheroe knew it was one of the most expensive iPads, so he knew it wasn't Merlin's, as his tablet was small and rather well-worn, being a refurbished Takaichi, a make nobody ever seemed to have heard of.

"Look at this," exclaimed Merlin excitedly. "I found this in the kitchen, and there was no password protection, so I thought I'd have a look and see whether there was anything interesting on it."

DI Protheroe went to look at the tablet. He realised he needn't worry about the assembled guests, as they had returned to tucking into the sumptuous buffet and chatting amongst themselves.

Merlin had found the iPad set at a particular page. It was clearly Miss Snyder's prepared speech, which was to have been read before the consumption of the buffet commenced. DI Protheroe started to read it.

"Well, first, I'd like to thank all of you for coming, as the evening just wouldn't have been the same without you all, and I mean all of you … although I am sure that your attendance is wholly because of the splendid and extremely expensive buffet that will soon be arriving. And you can be assured that it will be coming soon, as you know I am always 100% honest at all times.

And it is because of my innate honesty that I am taking this opportunity to tell you all a few home truths about yourselves. I have only been working at Daneman and Appleby for a few short years ... although it seemed to me to be an almost interminable period of time ... and I am now off to take up a prestigious post in probably the most important banking company in the City ... of London, that is, not the poor little backwater of Cardiff, which I began to detest on the day I arrived here.

But I have never felt happy here, and I have grown to loathe some of my so-called colleagues, with their petty secrets, their little affairs, their thievery, and their oh-so-futile little lives.

I was going to send all this information out to those in the office in an anonymous newsletter, but, when this job offer came up, I decided to go out in a blaze of glory ... although all the glory would be entirely for my own personal enjoyment.

So, let's start with my boss, Harry Andrews, who, and I am sure nobody else in the office knows, has been having an affair with little Belinda Makepiece in Accounts for the last five years. And yes, my dear, I'm sure he's ready to dump you instead of leaving his wife, as you're now insisting he does ... futilely, as I have no doubt.

And I have an email admitting that poor Gerry Cameron has been yet again passed over for promotion by his boss Jerry Fieldhouse. And the reason of course is that he's coloured. He has no chance, has he, Mr. Fieldhouse? There again, he may now, now that I have the proof for him ...

And I also have proof that Julie Braithwaite murdered her mother. I know everybody suspected that, but felt that it was a "mercy killing," as I believe it's known, but it was just a simple murder for Julie, purely to enable her to get her hands on her inheritance. Again, I have proof.

And little Molly Porter, or should I say, Maggie Prance, who now demonstrates the most extreme adherence to the rules of health and hygiene, with her little food-handler's gloves that she seems to wear at all times. I often wonder whether she takes them off when she visits the toilets in the office ... But who would have guessed that she was once solely responsible for half the staff in the office where she previously worked going down with food poisoning and one actually dying? I don't know to what degree the police got involved, but she tried to evade justice by changing her name. I really doubt that all this appears on the CV that she submitted to her current employers."

DI Protheroe read through the rest of the list, which accused each of the twelve office-workers assembled there with the most heinous crimes and adulteries, all allegedly with proof.

At the end, he read, "And finally, I come to dear little Dwayne Crump, the last on the list and the least likely to ever amount to anything … especially since he's stolen at least three laptops from the office, and that's just in the last three months. Anyway, I'd now like you to relax and enjoy the buffet. I am assured it will be splendid and will certainly not upset you, although, after my little speech, I'm sure each of you already has a bad taste in the mouth. Oh, and don't worry about attacking me or stealing my iPad, as I have backup copies, and all the relevant proofs have already been despatched to the, shall we say, soon-to-be-interested parties, that is, the wives, the board of directors at Daneman and Appleby's parent company … oh, and, where applicable, the police. I thank you!"

DI Protheroe looked up and sighed. He now had a whole hall full of people with a motive for killing Miss Snyder.

"But who would have had a chance to read this?" muttered Merlin to his brother.

"And, if they had read it to the end, they would have realised that such a murder would be pointless, if Miss Snyder had been telling the truth about having sent off the evidence, as I am sure she was."

DI Protheroe made a quick visit back to the main hall, where he learnt that Miss Snyder had carried her enormous handbag, which habitually contained her iPad, all evening, right up until the time she had gone into the kitchen to collect the cake and presumably to set up the iPad prior to making her speech. A few of those assembled there said she had been even more protective of her handbag than usual.

And, as it was a warm night, nobody had any need to wear gloves.

DI Protheroe retired to the kitchen once again, to think things over. He was a bit worried about individually interviewing everyone as it was getting quite late.

However, for the time being, everybody was quite happy to be left alone to chat and continue eating their way through the large amount of food provided. Little did they know how close they had come to having their enjoyment of the whole evening ruined by Miss Snyder's speech, although, if Miss Snyder's threats of public denouncement were genuine, next day's suffering would be far worse than the Bollinger-induced hangovers.

After a few minutes' thought, Merlin suggested his brother might only need to interview one person.

He suggested, "You know, this may in fact be a rather simple case."

"Firstly, there is only one person who could have seen the iPad, as Miss Snyder only opened it when she went into the kitchen to collect the cake and prepare for her speech."

"Secondly, it's a warm night, so nobody here had any need to wear gloves."

DI Protheroe nodded, and said, "Yes, I just checked and nobody seems to have any."

Merlin continued, "I've asked around a little, and it seems that only Miss Snyder's assistant, Molly Porter, went with her into the kitchen to collect the cake. If the iPad were set up alongside the cake so that Miss Snyder's speech would be ready, only Miss Porter could have read part of it and assimilated its basic points, although not the fact that the evidence had already been sent out to be made public. Also, as she was what she would no doubt call a "catering professional," she would have insisted on using her little disposable gloves in case she were asked to handle the cake, not that Miss Snyder would have bothered, although I am sure she would have been mortified if anyone had died of food poisoning and escaped her retribution."

"So, Miss Snyder must have gone into the toilets to get herself ready for her big speech. Not having time to communicate the iPad's contents to anyone else in the hall, Molly must have followed her and stabbed her to keep her quiet. The knife would have mainly had Miss Snyder's prints on, if Molly had indeed worn her little gloves …"

Merlin opened the waste bin in the kitchen. "And here they are, complete, I hope, with lots of DNA to link to Molly and the knife."

"I see why they call you 'The Wizard,'" said his brother.

But he was only trying to butter him up so that he would be happy to help on future cases.

Case 2023/004

Behind the Times

"And he's going to get away with it," said Miriam Horton indignantly.

"I know James Moffat stabbed my husband. I know he did it. But the police say he has a cast-iron alibi …"

"Hold on a second," said Merlin Protheroe. "Would you care to start at the beginning?" He leant back in the swivel chair in his office and tried to adopt an intellectual pose. "Well," he thought, "It might work …"

"Well, it was the evening of New Year's Day. My husband, Gareth, and a few friends were at a local pub. It wasn't one of those with a bad reputation, but it was ironic that they had tried to avoid the busy New Year's Eve celebrations in case things got out of hand. I suppose they were just unlucky to be there at that time. A fight started out on the pavement, and poor Gareth, who was only trying to break it up, got stabbed. He said it was James Moffat, and all his friends said the same. But the police have been hoodwinked into believing he was miles away at the time."

"He said he had been with friends in a pub in West Wales, in the Fishguard area. And everyone in the pub said he had been there celebrating with them for the whole of New Year's Day."

"So the police said we must have been mistaken ... but Gareth and his friends can't all have made the same mistake. It couldn't have been Moffat, the police said. But I know it was. And it looks as if they've decided it's not worth proceeding with the case unless there's new evidence."

"It took them a while, about a fortnight, to track him down. He'd been travelling around West Wales. He's unemployed, probably unemployable, so he'd been sponging off friends, if I know him."

"Anyway, he got everybody in the pub and those celebrating with him to give him an alibi for the whole of New Year's Day, and, even if they lost sight of him for an hour or so, he could hardly have travelled from West Wales to Penarth and back again in such a short space of time."

"So, the police let him off the hook."

"But I know it was him ..."

Merlin nodded. "I have an idea."

"But I have two questions."

"Firstly, was the name of the West Wales pub the Dyffryn Arms?"

Miriam nodded, "Oh yes, I could hardly forget something like that, after the whole pub lied that Moffat had been there all that day, could I? How did you know? Has it got a bad reputation?"

Merlin smiled, "Oh no, not at all."

"And secondly, who went to interview the people in the Dyffryn Arms? Was it the local police force there, or did they send someone up from Penarth?"

"Two detectives travelled up from Penarth. They even spent the night in the area. I think they thought of it as a night out. And they still didn't get any evidence against Moffat."

Merlin nodded. "In this case at least, I think the local police force might have been more effective."

"As I said, I have an idea. I have some influence with the police ..." (he was thinking of his brother, who was a Detective Inspector) "... And I think I can straighten this out."

"So, his friends *were* lying about his being in West Wales on New Year's Day, then?" asked Miriam Horton hopefully.

"Oh no. They weren't lying," replied Merlin enigmatically. "The Welsh are a very truthful race."

"Leave it with me."

-oOo-

The case had not been closed but had been left dormant as it was deemed unlikely that further information would be forthcoming.

But, after Merlin's suggestion, it was reopened, and James Moffat was arrested and charged.

"You see," said Merlin when Miriam Horton returned to his office, "The people in the Dyffryn Arms weren't lying when they said he was there for the whole of New Year's Day. And Moffat was counting on their honesty."

"It's just that they do things differently in the Gwaun Valley, and the Dyffryn Arms is at the centre of things. They still stick to the Julian calendar there …"

Miriam Horton raised her eyebrows as she felt that surprise on her part was expected, but, in fact, she had no real idea what Merlin was talking about.

"Yes, they follow the Julian Calendar, named after Julius Caesar, not the Gregorian calendar that we follow. So they celebrate New Year's Day, Hen Galan, on January the thirteenth."

"Children roam the countryside singing carols in return for the reward of calennig, sweets or money, and the menfolk take the Mari Lwyd, a horse's skull on a pole, or nowadays only a representation of one, around the houses chanting and singing, and expecting hospitality if their banter is not reciprocated."

"Er, what has this to do with my Gareth?" asked Miriam Horton, clearly under the impression she was being treated to some sort of travelogue.

"Your husband's attacker, may have been in the Gwaun Valley on New Year's Day, but that was on January the thirteenth, not January the first, when your husband was attacked."

"So, his alibi has evaporated."

Miriam Horton smiled for the first time in months.

Case 2023/005

Pier Pressure

"Did you see that?" screamed the man by the telescope.

Merlin Protheroe was taking a morning promenade along Penarth Esplanade. To his left were a few restaurants and the Italian Gardens, and, to the right, the Bristol Channel, now at high tide. The rise and fall of the tides here was the second largest in the world.

Projecting out elegantly from the Esplanade was the Victorian pier, opened in 1898, with its splendid 1929 art deco pavilion.

And it was on this pier that the man who had shouted had focused the telescope. It was one of those coin-in-the-slot telescopes often provided at seaside resorts.

"Did you see that?" he yelled again. His accent suggested he was a tourist from the London area.

Merlin looked towards him. "A guy just walked right up to the railings at the very end of the pier, tied a rope from his neck to the railings, shouted out something, and just jumped over. Come on!"

Merlin doubted that the loud gentleman wanted to go and see if he could help in any way. Rather he seemed the type of person who causes long traffic jams on motorways when there has been an accident of some sort on the other carriageway.

But Merlin wasn't that sort of person. He had listened to what had happened, but was sure there were enough people there to help, if any help were needed, but there was another possibility that had occurred to him, and so he decided to wait on the Esplanade and watch the pier for a minute or two ...

The apparent-suicide must have vaulted a railing to the area at the farthest point of the pier, from where the last-seagoing passenger-carrying paddle steamer in the world, the Waverley, made its way in the tourist season around the Bristol Channel. The pier was 650 feet long, with plenty of more accessible points along its length. And there were plenty of people about, tourists, young mothers with prams, fishermen, the more elderly just sauntering along ...

What had occurred to Merlin was that it was odd that the apparent suicide had decided to jump from the very end of the pier, rather than from the sides, where there was more space and the railings were more accessible. But perhaps he was really serious and felt that jumping from the end of the pier might mean that there would be a longer delay in anybody trying to stop or save him.

But, contradicting that, it was also a very public way in which he had carried out the act. There would have been times when there were fewer people about, but, at this time of day, the whole place was alive with people.

So, Merlin waited a little while and let others rush to the end of the pier. He felt he would only be in the way anyway.

And then he saw someone wade out of the water underneath the pier and walk up the beach to the steps leading to the Esplanade.

Although he was, naturally, soaking wet, he made no attempt to stop and dry himself, but just crossed the road on the pedestrian crossing and entered Alexandra Park.

Merlin decided to follow this erstwhile swimmer. He phoned his sister Guinevere on his mobile and said in which direction they were moving.

After Alexandra Park, Merlin's quarry entered Windsor Road, the main shopping area in Penarth. But Merlin began to suspect he knew he was being followed, as he entered the local Bonmarché. One of the unusual features of this store was that its main entrance was in Windsor Road, but there was another, smaller, public entrance to the rear, in Ludlow Lane.

Perhaps the quarry hoped that Merlin didn't know the area well, but Merlin was pretty sure what he was trying to do, and went around the block via Albert Road, and caught sight of the man as he left the rear entrance. He was able to take a photograph too.

He then followed the man back to Arcot Street, where he noted which house he entered.

Merlin hadn't been hired by anybody, especially not by anybody who would be paying him.

Nevertheless, he thought it was time to get in touch with his brother, DI Arthur Protheroe.

He was certainly interested in Merlin's story.

And the investigation was so easy.

Dennis Murray had got into bad gambling debts. He had cleared these with a loan from Henry Crabtree, a small, rather insignificant little man he felt he need not fear, but, when someone resembling a domestic mercenary whom the moneylender had hired called around with unveiled threats, Murray knew he had to sort the situation out, drastically if necessary.

So, he had arranged to meet up with Henry Crabtree in order to pay off his debts, or so he said. A public place suited Henry Crabtree.

But Murray had given him a sedative, had supported him to the end of the pier and had then tied a rope around his neck and tied it to the railings. When he felt sure nobody was looking, he threw him over the edge. Then he made sure everybody *was* looking, tied a rope around his own neck (but not to the railings) and jumped over the railings himself. Then he swam ashore.

There was plenty of evidence on the railings. Dennis Murray had clearly not expected anybody to suspect murder and had been careless.

Case 2023/006

Hair Apparent

"When we get a conviction there, it'll have to be by reason of insanity," proclaimed PC Watkins.

"Eh?" said Detective Inspector Arthur Protheroe, deep in thought.

"I mean, why is Bernard denying that he killed his father? We have all the evidence we need, even photographs."

DI Protheroe and PC Watkins had just paid a visit to Bernard Curtis-Brown in his small cottage in the middle of the Vale of Glamorgan countryside.

The previous evening, his father, Gerald, had been shot in his local pub, the 'Crooked Brewer.' This was in front of a number of witnesses, some of whom had taken some rather high-definition photographs on their mobile phones.

And Bernard Curtis-Brown had a rather striking appearance. His fluffy blond hair, a small neat moustache and a small scar on his cheek, together with his height of six foot four, seem to match perfectly the photographs DI Protheroe and PC Watkins had been shown. But, even when shown the photographs himself, Curtis-Brown refused to accept that it was he who had been photographed.

"I was in all night, watching television," he claimed, although he could not back this up.

And there were few suspects, simply Bernard, his sister and her husband. All of them needed money, as the children of rich people always seem to, and none had a good alibi. Harold Porter, Bernard's brother-in-law, maintained he had been with his wife all evening, although DI Protheroe and PC Watkins both thought that she would have agreed to anything her husband said. However, she herself seemed too small and weak to have matched the description of the murderer.

"Just look at these photographs," muttered PC Watkins. "You can clearly see it's Bernard Curtis-Brown. And three witnesses said he had to duck when leaving, so, as I've been in that pub and I know how high the door is, he must have been around six foot four. And all that makes Bernard our murderer."

DI Protheroe moved his head noncommittally. "We had better see if the landlord has got that CCTV footage ready," he said and headed for the car.

-oOo-

The 'Crooked Brewer' was one of those old village pubs which had been turned into a gastropub with the concomitant increase in prices to cover the pretension. Before the grand reopening, it had been known as the 'Rose and Crown,' but that was deemed too traditional for the pub's new character.

The landlord, George Murray, had also upgraded the CCTV system, and the images were as clear as those from the customers' phones.

The victim was sitting alone at a table in the bar and was readily identifiable. Suddenly, a tall gentleman entered the bar, sought out his target, and then shot him at very close range. His appearance tallied with that in the phone images: he had fluffy blond hair, a neat moustache and a scar on his cheek. He then turned and ambled out of the bar, ducking to avoid knocking his head against the lintel.

"There," said PC Watkins, a little irritably, "It's clearly Bernard. Everything fits. Who else would it be?"

DI Protheroe demurred, "I have a feeling Bernard's lawyer might raise a few objections, some valid. For instance, the assailant's hair is somehow bigger and isn't in quite the same style, his moustache is a little bigger, and the scar is in a slightly different position."

PC Watkins looked a little shocked and not at all convinced.

DI Protheroe continued, "And I also noticed his left foot twisted at one point, as if he were wearing shoes he wasn't used to."

PC Watkins tutted.

"And there's another set of CCTV footage from the path leading away from the pub entrance."

DI Protheroe played the video.

It clearly showed the tall gentleman leaving the pub and wobbling down the path to the roadway. He took off the wig he was wearing and dropped a bag into a nearby rubbish bin.

DI Protheroe was waiting for PC Watkins to start spluttering some comments in defence of his theory of Bernard's culpability, but he just said "Oh," rather disappointedly.

"We must check that rubbish bin and get whatever was dumped in there checked for DNA. And I think we need to interview the victim's family more fully."

-oOo-

If DI Protheroe had decided he would need to interview the victim's family more fully, he reasoned it would also be a good idea to involve his own family too.

There were already a number of things that worried him about the case, and he was sure his brother, Merlin, would be of at least some small assistance. He was suggesting to himself that he could use his brother as a sounding-board, so he could pitch his ideas to him for his consideration, but, in reality, he knew it would be his brother who would come up with ideas and theories and, ultimately, solutions.

After picking up Merlin, DI Protheroe collected the bag from the bin at the 'Crooked Brewer.' It contained a blond wig. He delivered it to Forensics, and then drove on to Harold Porter's house.

Harold Porter invited DI Protheroe into his lounge and sat alongside his wife, Maddy. He was an out-of-work actor, but he was honest enough not the use the oft-used euphemism "resting."

In answer to DI Protheroe's queries, he replied, "Well, I stick to my alibi … my wife bears that out …" Maddy nodded quietly, "… But, having had a phone call from my esteemed brother-in-law, I don't think that will be needed. As you can see, I am five-foot ten and almost completely bald." He smiled almost apologetically.

"And would your father-in-law have had any enemies?"

"Hardly. He was a retired and well-respected accountant. He was rich, but his money was inherited from his father. I don't think he stepped on any toes in his career, and he certainly didn't need to take out any loans from the Mafia."

DI Protheroe checked that he agreed for a DNA team to call later that day to check both Harold and his wife.

-oOo-

Bernard Curtis-Brown again stuck to his story. He also agreed to a DNA check.

-oOo-

The results of the DNA tests were unexpected.

There was not the slightest DNA match between any of the family members and the contents of the bag.

"Well, the killer was wearing gloves," said DI Protheroe, "… But there should have been some evidence on the wig at least."

He lapsed into silence.

"I suppose we'll now have to delve into the victim's background and find out whether he did have any enemies."

-oOo-

But there seemed to be nobody who could be classed as an enemy, except perhaps the family.

-oOo-

"Not as good as the 'Blue Anchor,' is it?" said Merlin, looking around the "snug" at the 'Crooked Brewer.' It certainly didn't feel very snug. And neither did the prices.

DI Protheroe sat back. It was time to marshal his thoughts and present the details of the case to his brother for him to hopefully unravel the situation. He supposed it didn't matter that much how he presented things, as he knew his brother would fill in any gaps with a plethora of questions afterwards.

Merlin listened, perhaps a little distractedly, and then asked to see the CCTV footage.

Then he summarised the case, as he saw it.

"OK, so we have a murder victim, whom nobody seemed to want dead except his immediate family, and that only for financial reasons. He was murdered by someone who appeared to be trying to give the impression that the murderer was the victim's son, Bernard. He wore a wig similar to Bernard's own hair, and had a scar and a moustache, both of which may very well have been false, especially as the moustache was too large and the scar was not exactly in the right position. Also, the killer appeared to be of the same height as Bernard, but appeared unsteady on his feet, as if he were wearing built-up shoes."

"We know he was wearing a wig as he took it off outside the pub and a wig was found dumped in a nearby bin. But there was no DNA on it that could be linked to either of the three family members. And nobody else seems to have wanted Gerald dead."

"So, where are we?"

Thankfully, DI Protheroe realised that this question was rhetorical, and made no attempt at a reply … or perhaps he just had absolutely no idea what was going on.

"Right! I have not one, but two possible solutions. But which is the right one? Do I go with my gut feeling, or do we investigate further?"

There was a silence for a few minutes, sufficiently long for DI Protheroe to wonder whether he was expected to make a contribution to the conversation himself, when Merlin started up again.

"Right. Firstly, the DNA evidence. What if the killer took off his wig, but then dumped a different bag containing another wig into the rubbish bin? He was wearing gloves, so that would mean there would be no relevant DNA evidence."

"Secondly, I am not convinced that the killer was not six foot four. I agree that he seemed rather wobbly on his feet in the pub and on the path leading to the road, but that could be just acting, to throw us off the scent. But, if he had been a shorter man wearing built-up shoes, would he have known to duck before leaving through the door? I feel that, if our murderer were really six foot four, he would be used to anticipating low entrances and ducking … as indeed he did."

"And thirdly, I wondered why anybody would try to incriminate Bernard so well but would choose a wig that was not quite of the same style and a moustache that was much bigger, as well as positioning a scar on his cheek that was not quite in the right place."

"So, having had a look at the CCTV, which was, thankfully, high definition, and, looking closely at the assailant's face, I could just make out another scar, just to the left of the more obvious one. And make-up had clearly been applied to try to hide this other scar."

"And that smaller scar exactly matched that on Bernard's face."

"So, Arthur, what we have here is a son who wanted to kill his father for financial reasons, and who decided to disguise himself as himself, although rather badly …"

"The CCTV would prove that the killer was wearing a wig, and his strange gait would suggest someone wearing special shoes to make himself look taller. With his brother-in-law's acting background, suspicion would naturally fall onto Harold Porter."

"And, if that attempt failed, the lack of DNA evidence on the wig would suggest that an outsider were involved."

"Clever, eh? I think you need to go and have a long talk with Mr. Bernard Curtis-Brown."

Case 2023/007

Is This a Dagger?

"It just has to be some sort of conspiracy," wailed Ada Humphreys.

That comment came as a complete surprise to Merlin Protheroe, as the dear old lady seemed the last sort of person to espouse any conspiracy theories.

Merlin prompted her to continue.

"Well, I've always liked that actor David Whitbread. He's a local boy and I've followed his career since he was in plays at the school where I taught. And he's done very well for himself. He's been in the West End, although the play was cancelled after a week, and he's been in adverts on television, and, oh, lots of things."

"Anyway, last night he was in 'Macbeth' at the Paget Rooms ... playing Macbeth himself!"

The Paget Rooms was a Grade II listed theatre in Victoria Road, Penarth, which had opened in 1906. At various stages in its life it had been a dance hall and a cinema, but it was now owned by the local town council and used as a theatre and occasional location for films such as 'Submarine' and television series such as 'Sex Education.'

"It's currently touring the country. Now, I don't normally go to see things like Shakespeare, but, well, it was David Whitbread, so I booked a ticket. It was awful!"

Merlin nodded. "Yes, a lot of people don't like Shakespeare."

"Oh no, the play and the acting were fine, although I'm not sure what a purist would have thought of it. It was a modern reinterpretation, presumably to appeal to those who weren't fans of the Bard. So, it was set in modern times and Macbeth was an estate agent in a firm called 'Macduff and Company.' He gradually clawed his way up the hierarchy of the firm until it was 'Macbeth and Macduff,' in that order."

"And then Macduff killed his partner."

"Oh, it was so horrific. I thought it was acting at first, as David is such a fine thespian, but, when I saw all the blood, I knew it was for real."

"Anyway, they asked "Is there a doctor in the house?" I thought that only happened in films. But there was one, as luck would have it. He made a brief examination and then called for an ambulance. I just sat there with my heart in my mouth, as the blue flashing light from the ambulance lit up the auditorium. Then a police constable appeared and, a few minutes later, a detective arrived. They took down all the details and asked for witnesses. Of course I rushed forward …. there weren't many people in the audience, this being Shakespeare ... and gave my details, which were duly noted. I told them it was Macduff who had done it. The detective inspector said it always was, in the play, so I told him that I meant that the murderer was the *actor* playing Macduff. He seemed a little confused."

"And?" prompted Merlin.

"Well, I looked in all the newspapers this morning ... and online ... and on the television, and nowhere was there any mention of the fate of poor David. Was he mortally wounded? Was he only injured? Nobody seems to care. Everyone is trying to cover it all up, mark my words."

"But I am confident that you can find out the truth," said Ada Humphreys.

She sat back triumphantly.

"Well," stuttered Merlin, "I suppose it could be that the stage management or the theatre company might be worried that they would be liable under some health and safety ruling. Or perhaps everyone is trying to suppress the truth in order to keep the attacker's name secret."

"I shall start investigating for you immediately," he said, also sitting back triumphantly.

Mrs. Ada Humphreys announced her gratification at this, and left, clearly much happier than when she had arrived.

-oOo-

Merlin was lucky enough to have the chance to talk to Hayman Wiseacre, the director of Artychoke, the theatre company that was putting on the modern version of Macbeth "at selected venues around the country," although in fact it was usually wherever there was a cheap hall to hire. He was about to depart for Aylesbury, where the next performance would be put on later that week.

But, in reply to Merlin's queries about the whereabouts and well-being of David Whitbread, he would only smile evasively. "Check with the police if you're not happy," he said.

Similar enquiries of the police and of the local media yielded no results either.

Perhaps no-one would be the wiser until the next performance, when Macbeth might be played by an injured David Whitbread or by another actor entirely … or perhaps the whole run would be cancelled.

-oOo-

Merlin was sitting in his office ruminating. Guinevere was at her desk.

He explained the situation to her. Sometimes she could more easily see the solution, not having Merlin's cryptic mind.

"Have you tried their website?" she asked.

Merlin replied, "Well, I have glanced at it, but only to see if it contained any up-to-date news about David Whitbread, which it didn't."

"No, Merlin, have you looked at their description of their Macbeth play, or indeed of any of their previous plays? And have you checked for any critics' reviews of the previous performances of Macbeth?"

Merlin didn't shake his head but got onto that straight away.

-oOo-

Ada Humphreys climbed the stairs to Merlin's office after his phone call to her. She stopped for breath for a few seconds and then knocked on the door.

Merlin beamed at her.

"Well, Mrs. Humphreys, we've managed to answer your query."

"And is darling David OK?" came the reply.

Merlin smiled. "He's fine. He will be starring as Macbeth in the next production at Aylesbury, and without any injuries."

"But I saw him stabbed with a long knife, and there was a doctor there … and two ambulancemen … and two policemen … and such a lot of fuss."

Merlin nodded. "I can imagine how distressing it must have been for you."

"But I realised we should look at the theatre company's previous performances and the critics' reviews of them." He didn't look at Guinevere, who he knew would be scowling at him.

"Artychoke specialises in modern versions of classic plays …"

"Oh, I know all that," spluttered Mrs. Humphreys.

"… But presented so that the audience feels part of the story and feels similar emotions to the characters in the play. The whole play is acted out for real. So you were meant to be shocked at the very realistic murder of David Whitbread, or rather, Macbeth. But it was all faked, for effect."

"So, he's OK?"

"Yes, I can assure you he's fine. I know one or two would-be actors in South Wales, so I was able to check which digs were currently popular in the

Penarth area. David Whitbread no longer seems to have any family around here, so he would need to find accommodation. I checked on the most likely addresses and managed to locate him. So, at the moment, he is still in Penarth, safe and sound and entirely unharmed."

"Oh, that is a relief," said Mrs. Humphreys who had clearly been holding her breath, waiting to hear the results of Merlin's investigation.

Suddenly, the office door opened.

Mrs. Humphreys turned around expectantly, but it was only the postman, who dumped a few bills on Guinevere's desk and then left.

She looked so disappointed.

Case 2023/008

I Spy

Jayne Jaynes phoned up Merlin Protheroe one Thursday morning.

"I have a problem," she admitted.

"That's why people come to me, for me to sort out their problems," replied Merlin with more confidence than was justified.

"It's a little complicated," said Mrs. Jaynes, for she must have been married, as Merlin was certain not only that that had not been her name at birth, but also that she must have really loved her husband.

"I live in Clinton Road, Penarth, and was driving in Cogan today when I had an altercation with someone, not a very nice man. He was rather rough and uncouth, and he looked like some sort of down-and-out. He accused me of driving too close to his son, who was about four years old, I suppose, and who had wandered into the road in front of me. The boy was clearly not under any sort of control at all, but I was certainly nowhere near hitting him. His father screamed and ranted at me, and then he threatened me."

"He said he'd get even with me, even if it was the last thing he ever did. He said he knew where I lived."

"This worried me so much I returned to my friend's house … the one I had just been visiting … and told her what had happened, and she recognised this man from my description."

"So I know who he is. In fact, I think everybody in Cogan knows him because of his bad attitude and coarse behaviour. I'm surprised he has a house at all, let alone a son."

"Anyway, the police didn't seem interested as no crime had yet been committed, and so I'd like you to watch him tonight. That's when I feel sure he'll carry out his threat, as I'm sure he means to."

"And this is his name and address."

She handed over a sheet of paper with the name Harry Oldman, and an address in Cogan.

"Well," continued Merlin, "There are some things I am allowed to do and some I'm not. I can legally follow someone around, as long as I'm not breaking any privacy laws, such as photographing people through the windows of their house or in their back garden. But I'm sure I can handle this for you."

Mrs Jaynes thanked him and left the office.

Merlin sat back in his chair and thought about the case.

-oOo-

That night, Merlin sat in his car in a side street in Cogan. His sister, Guinevere, had insisted that his plans to have advertisements about his job plastered all over his car would make it unsuitable for surveillance purposes, and Merlin now conceded to himself that this had been a sensible decision.

He had with him a flask of hot coffee, black and sweet and syrupy, to try and keep him awake, a pair of binoculars that a relative had found insufficient for his birdwatching hobby, and a notebook. Having considered and assessed what Mrs. Jaynes had said, he expected a fruitless wait.

But he was wrong. At one o'clock precisely, Mr. Oldman left his house and drove off in a battered old Transit van.

He didn't seem to consider that someone might be tailing him, and drove straight to an address, not in Clinton Road, where Mrs. Jaynes lived, but in Plymouth Road, a fairly long street leading south from the town centre, and full of large and rather grand three-storey Victorian semi-detached houses.

He must have already discovered that the occupants were away, because he made no checks, but immediately broke a side window and entered the house. He made a few journeys bringing stuff out and stashing it in his van, and then he drove home.

And Merlin had it all on camera.

-oOo-

Detective Inspector Arthur Protheroe, Merlin's brother, was naturally very interested in the photographs and was sure the case against Harry Oldman would be a simple one.

Merlin felt he had good news for Mrs. Jaynes.

-oOo-

"So I don't think Mr. Oldman will be bothering you now. He has enough on his plate with the charges that the police will be bringing against him."

Mrs. Jaynes seemed relieved. She thanked him, paid his account, and left, apparently satisfied.

Merlin sat back and thought.

-oOo-

Merlin began to feel that he was being taken for a ride. Hardly any of the cases he was given seemed simple. It always seemed that he wasn't being told the truth, or at least not the whole truth.

And he was sure that this was one of those cases.

He hadn't completely believed the reason why Mrs. Jaynes said she was hiring him. It all seemed a little too contrived. And why would a rough, uncouth fellow in Cogan know where Mrs. Jaynes lived? Or was this just an idle threat and his client had overreacted?

If she had contacted the police about the threats, he wasn't sure that her claims would have been noted down by whoever received her enquiry, if indeed she had reported the threats.

But perhaps …

He got through to his brother again, who was now slightly in his debt after Merlin had provided the evidence about Harry Oldman's nighttime activities.

And he was told that Mrs. Jaynes had indeed filed a report of a crime, but not of threats …

Mrs. Jaynes had been the victim of a burglary. She had had stolen, amongst other items, a DVD-recorder, which a friend of hers had recovered by buying it when it was offered for sale in a local pub. He had bought it to replace the one she had had stolen, but she was able to confirm that it was indeed hers.

So Merlin had a chat with the landlord of the pub.

And he was then able to piece together what had actually happened.

The landlord, another friend, had confided in her the name and address of the person who had sold the

DVD-recorder. He said he often had things to sell on a Friday evening. Perhaps, he ventured, he was in the habit of burgling houses on Thursday evenings.

And Mrs. Jaynes had wanted to get her revenge ...

Case 2023/009

On the Scent

Angela Evans phoned Merlin Protheroe at his office and asked him to call around. Things were quiet so he called around almost immediately.

Miss Evans lived in a terraced house in Plassey Street. She was young, twenty-five years old or so, with straggly blonde hair, wearing jeans with a tear at the knee and a baggy jumper.

Merlin immediately assumed she was an untidy, rather scruffy individual, but revised his opinion when he saw the interior of her house. He supposed that her clothing must just have been trendy, not that Merlin would have known that, but the house was immaculate, with everything neatly put away, no sign of dust, and a degree of cleanliness that only just fell short of OCD.

"So, what's the problem?" asked Merlin.

"Well, it's a little difficult to explain. I'm very well-organised and believe there's no point in owning anything unless you know where it is and can find it when you need it, so I knew immediately when I returned home yesterday that I'd been burgled. The house was a little dishevelled, shall we say. Only slightly so, though, but I am absolutely 100% certain that someone had broken into my house."

"Did you contact the police?" asked Merlin, knowing exactly what the reply would be.

"Well, of course, but as nothing of any real value had been taken, they were hardly interested."

"So, something was taken?"

"Yes, a large bottle of perfume. It had no real value, I mean, it wasn't one of those really expensive bottles costing thousands, but it had been given to me by a fairly well-off boyfriend when I was at university, and it had been created and conceived especially for me. It was very personal. Er, it was labelled 'Evans' Scent'"

"And had there been any forced entry?"

"Oh no, nothing was damaged. But someone had been into my bedroom and had looked through my clothes. They had been put back fairly tidily, but not tidily enough for me not to know someone had been browsing through them."

"Oh, and I'm not stupid. I fully realise that this seems nonsensical."

Merlin nodded, but said nothing.

"Does anybody else have a key to the place? I assume it's your house, not rented."

"It's my house, and nobody else has any financial interest in it, apart from the bank, not that there are any left in Penarth anymore."

"But my boyfriend has my spare key, I suppose in case I should ever lose mine, not that I ever would be so careless … I certainly never have done. But I have asked him, and I am 100% certain that he was telling the truth when he said that he isn't the one who broke in."

"I'm sure he wasn't the one," replied Merlin, "But I'd better have a chat with him."

Angela provided his address.

-oOo-

Harry Davies lived in a semi-detached house in Dinas Powys, not too far away. He was quite happy to chat about Angela.

"Yes, our relationship is very good, although I'm a little unsure about a long-term commitment at this stage. And Angela mentioned that she thought she might have been burgled, but only some perfume was stolen, so she may have been mistaken. Perhaps she mislaid the bottle. It's not as if it was an expensive perfume. But I definitely did not break into Angela's house, and I did not lend my key to anyone."

Merlin thought for a while. Then he asked, "And is there anybody else who you're romantically linked to or who might want to replace Angela in your affections?"

Harry Davies shook his head. "No, it's only Angela I want …"

But he seemed a little thoughtful.

Merlin persevered …

-oOo-

Having got a name out of Harry Davies, Merlin decided on the direct approach.

He called around to meet Jane Martin at her flat in Penarth.

"So, where is that bottle of perfume, Miss Martin?"

It didn't take long for her to admit that she'd taken a chance and "borrowed" Harry Davies' copy of Angela Evans' key. She had used it to look around Angela's house, to check on her taste in clothes and perfume. But, as the perfume was unique, she felt she had to steal it ...

… because she was desperate to become Harry Davies' steady girlfriend instead of Angela Evans. And she reasoned that the best way was to learn what she could about her rival's style and taste, and copy them, including using her unique perfume.

"I suppose I've really messed up my chances with Harry now," she said sadly.

Merlin said nothing.

Case 2023/010

Too Much Caffeine is Bad for You

"My fame is spreading," announced Merlin Protheroe proudly.

"Bristol? London? New York?" enquired his sister, Guinevere.

Merlin frowned. "Actually, Newport."

"But that's only about seventeen miles away."

"Well, it's a start. Sharon Butterworth is calling over in an hour or two."

-oOo-

"Do you undertake work following unfaithful husbands?" asked Sharon Butterworth.

"If you're paying, yes," said Merlin Protheroe, trying to be humorous, but a little worried in case he just sounded mercenary.

"Well, my husband, Leslie his name is, is, or I strongly suspect he is, is having an affair with a waitress at a coffee shop in Newport city centre."

Merlin reeled at the plethora of ises.

"What I want you to do is to wait in Long John's Coffee Shop each lunchtime from noon to two o'clock this week. It's a little way down from the first-floor office in which my husband works, but it's where he has lunch every day. I would try and follow him myself, but I'm not very good at covert operations, as I think they're called." She clearly watched a lot of dramas about soldiers or spies on television, or perhaps her husband did.

"Anyway, you can write your report whilst in there to save you time. I'm not worried about my husband in the evenings and weekends. He's with me then. But I have grave suspicions about his liaisons during weekday lunchtimes. You can start Monday. Oh, and I might ask you to verify your report in court, if necessary. Obviously, then I would pay any extra expenses and charges incurred."

Merlin nodded. She seemed very bossy, but, as long as she paid for his services, that was fine with him.

Monday at 11.50 a.m. found Merlin ensconced in Long John's. He was surprised that Mr. Butterworth used that coffee shop as there was another one right opposite the entrance to his place of work, but perhaps he felt that this one was the better of the two. And the whole town was full of coffee shops. Perhaps the entire local populace desperately needed something to perk themselves up every morning, although, considering the passers-by Merlin noticed through the coffee shop window, it didn't seem to be working.

But Leslie Butterworth seemed an ideal husband, or at least in terms of his having an affair. He diligently went through reports at his table whilst having a sandwich and a cup of coffee, and his attention never strayed. He certainly never looked at Merlin, and so presumably had no suspicion that he was being watched. There again, he hardly looked at the other patrons either.

Merlin noticed that he was only ever served by one of the two waitresses there. She was of medium height with dark hair and a fairly slim figure. But the reason was soon clear. She must have had seniority over the other girl, and always showed her delight at the tips she was given by Butterworth. The other girl was a little older with pink hair.

After five days of lunchtime surveillance, Merlin had seen nothing untoward, although he had not been having much sleep each night, not because his work was taxing, but because of his increased caffeine intake.

That Friday, Merlin completed his report whilst at the coffee table, and took it to Mrs. Butterworth. He felt he could allay any fears she had about her husband's infidelity, at least based on his observations, and presented his account, which was promptly settled.

And so it was that another case was successfully concluded by Merlin Protheroe.

And with no incriminations, arguments, upsets or disagreements. It was all very pleasant and financially rewarding, which is how Merlin liked his cases.

-oOo-

And yet he was not entirely happy about the case.

Leslie Butterworth had seemed the perfect husband and employee, working through his lunch hour (or two), ignoring the blandishments of the waitresses, tipping rather heavily, and yet having the most perfect demeanour. Had he known he was being watched and so put on a respectable facade for anyone watching? Had he discovered that his wife had hired someone to shadow him?

Merlin toyed with the idea of phoning Mrs. Butterworth and informing her of his suspicions, but, well, he had done as he was asked, and he didn't want to upset the marriage if it was indeed stable … and he didn't want to give the impression that he wanted more work and more money out of her.

Almost reluctantly, he decided to let the matter rest unless he were again contacted by Mrs. Butterworth … but he kept his mind open and avidly read any news from Newport.

-oOo-

It wasn't long before something attracted his attention in one of the Newport papers. It related to a death on the Friday, the last day Merlin had been watching Leslie Butterworth in Long John's coffee shop.

"On Friday afternoon, Chloe James, one of the waitresses at the Newport branch of the countrywide chain of Ishmael's Coffee Shops was found stabbed to death in the toilet at the rear of the shop. She was last seen working at 12.45 p.m., and was found at 1.10 p.m. in a locked toilet cubicle, after she had not appeared to help customers for some time. Her manageress, Shirley Higgins, described her as her best employee ever …"

Merlin had always noticed that, however villainous, deceitful or unpleasant people were, they were always alleged to be the most saintly upon their demise.

"… and she would be sorely missed. She had, however, seemed rather distracted of late, and may have been a little depressed ... A much-respected member of the local police force said investigations were continuing."

Merlin thought a little more. The manageress seemed to be trying to suggest suicide, perhaps because she felt that that was a better option than murder in terms of adverse publicity, although Merlin usually found that the notoriety of a murder having been committed on the premises increased business exponentially. Merlin had himself visited the toilets there after his Monday session, and he knew that the locks were very flimsy and could easily be opened or shut from the outside. But surely this could hardly relate to his own case, as Leslie Butterworth had been under his surveillance all the time from noon until two on the day of the murder, and he hadn't left his table at all during that time.

So he had a cast-iron alibi ...

... as provided, if requested, by Merlin.

He wondered if he had been unwittingly duped.

So, if he had been hired to give Leslie Butterworth an alibi, it was his wife who had set it all up. But why would she want dead a waitress from a different coffee shop to the one her husband frequented?

Despite no longer being employed (or paid), Merlin paid a visit to the Newport branch of Ishmael's where the unfortunate waitress had worked. A few enquiries were enough to confirm that this was the caffeine outlet that Leslie Butterworth actually visited regularly. And he had seemed to have enjoyed the attentions of poor Chloe James. Were they having an affair?

But, if so, why would Sharon Butterworth have so carefully set up her husband's alibi? And why would he have agreed to using a neighbouring coffee shop to create the alibi?

Merlin doubted that Sharon would have known how to arrange for a hired killer to despatch poor Chloe, and, either way, that only increased the dangers of being caught or blackmailed.

When the murder became public, her husband, if totally innocent, would have been suspicious (and worried about his own demise at his wife's hands, perhaps), so he must have been a willing partner in the affair.

Merlin had an idea. He did some research on the Butterworth family's background.

He phoned up his brother in the local police force and suggested he contact his opposite numbers in Newport. He told them what he was sure had happened and gave his evidence.

He suggested that the local force confirm the relationship between Chloe James and Leslie Butterworth; check on the movements of Sharon Butterworth's' car on the day of the murder, using CCTV cameras; check any CCTV cameras outside Ishmael's for proof that she parked nearby and visited the coffee shop at the relevant time; and try and obtain some DNA evidence from the clothes in her wardrobe, as there must have been some blood spilled, and Merlin hoped that Sharon Butterworth would have been so confident that her plan would succeed that she would have been a little careless in this regard.

The Police finally established that Chloe James had started blackmailing Leslie Butterworth about his relationship with her. But it wasn't his wife that she threatened to tell, but Leslie's ancient aunt, who was very religious and traditional. She had had to be consulted before Leslie's marriage in order to secure her approval.

So Leslie had confided all to his wife, who had decided on drastic action, not because she took his affair as a personal insult, but solely because she was desperate to ensure that they would continue to be the sole intended recipients of the Butterworth fortune ... and it was well-known that the aunt, Amelia Butterworth, was very keen on cats and supported the local cats' home, at this stage only infrequently.

Sharon Butterworth resolved that Chloe should be silenced once and for all. She had arranged the alibi with Merlin and had then murdered the girl herself.

It was still a few days before Merlin's sleep patterns returned to normal.

Back to the Drawing Board

A diversion

Early one Sunday morning, Guinevere Potts called around to see her brother and business partner, Merlin Protheroe, at his home. At one time she would often call around socially, but recently, as their business had begun to prosper, it was usually only on business matters.

Merlin was therefore surprised to find the visit wasn't concerning their detective agency.

"A friend of mine has started writing detective stories," she announced, rather self-consciously.

Merlin wondered if it were in fact Guinevere herself who was a budding Nick Fowler, Penarth's famous crime novelist.

"And she's written a detective story that's 'period.' It's set in the 1970s, and it's about a small town rugby team manager who's murdered on a coach after an away match."

"Will you read the first part and tell me what you think?"

Merlin nodded, albeit a little reluctantly.

"I'll go and make us a cup of tea and get some of those expensive chocolate biscuits you hide in the kitchen, shall I?" said Guinevere, clearly not even considering that there might be any objection on Merlin's part.

"You can skip the first two chapters, as they only set up the characters and the location. I only really want you to read the parts about the crime and the way it's solved. I haven't got all day to sit around here munching chocolate biscuits."

Merlin started reading from Chapter 3 …

-oOo-

Llangoch Rugby Club's away match to Mugby Junction had been rather an embarrassment, not that the team and the management had been expecting anything other than a loss. Their manager, Harry Cuthbert always said, "It's not the winning that counts, it's having a good match with fair and skilful play and with everyone enjoying themselves." But most players and supporters felt they could only enjoy themselves if they actually won the match, or at least felt that they had a chance of winning, or even perhaps if they scored just once …

The hospitality afterwards was more lavish than at most fixtures, purely because Llangoch was such a popular team, being 100% beatable. After the team had eaten and drunk freely they gradually returned to the coach.

There was no need for a large coach as a locally hired Bedford Plaxton 29-seater was sufficient for the team, management and all the supporters.

Harry Cuthbert, feeling a bit the worse for wear after all the drink he had imbibed, was the first on the coach, in fact at least five minutes before the others. He always liked to sit well away from the 'hoi polloi' of the rest of the club, although he only used this term to himself. If his views on the class system were known, there were plenty of other people in the club who would use this to kick him off the board. He was not well-liked as it was.

Harry always hired a larger coach from the same company for the annual works outing for the employees of his clothing factory in the Valleys ("It's not a sweat shop, but everyone is expected to work up at least a reasonable amount of perspiration"). And he always made sure that he made a good profit out of these trips. But he insisted on hiring a coach with a tip-up seat over the front step well. These were only intended to be used by couriers or co-drivers when travelling abroad, but it meant that Harry could get the profit from an extra seat and that he himself could occupy it so that he could sit separately from everyone else.

But the smaller 29-seater didn't feature a courier's seat. So Harry always took the front single seat for himself. At least he didn't have to endure the close proximity of the other members of the club.

Afterwards, the other twenty-eight members of the club (for every seat on the coach had been filled) said that Harry had been slumped in the single front seat as they passed him to get to the rear seats. They assumed he had fallen asleep whilst drunk.

As indeed he may have done … but he had also been stabbed to death, almost certainly by one of the club members getting on the coach after him. And most of those had boarded the vehicle separately rather than all together. This was because some stragglers had had to visit the toilets for varying periods of time before leaving (rather than the customary standing beside the coach in a lay-by somewhere), whilst others had taken the opportunity to fill their pockets with sausage rolls for the return journey or for the kids at home.

-oOo-

Merlin stopped reading.

"Er, Gwen, I think you have a problem here," he said.

Guinevere put down her chocolate biscuit.

"Eh?" she said, spraying Merlin with crumbs.

"I suppose it's an essential element of the story that Harry Cuthbert is sitting on his own on a single seat?"

"Yes," said Guinevere monosyllabically, as a fresh spray of crumbs headed in Merlin's direction.

"Well," continued Merlin, "I'm not sure what the configuration of seats is on today's coaches, but, in the 1970s, there wouldn't have been a single seat at the front."

"Oh, of course there would have been," argued Guinevere. "I've been on coaches myself, and there are always two seats on either side of the aisle … or sometimes three on one side and two on the other. So, there has to be a single seat at the front, because twenty-nine is an odd number. That's obvious, isn't it?"

She looked at Merlin as if she doubted his intelligence. She was probably wondering whether bringing the story to him had been a good idea in the first place.

"So," continued Merlin, "If you walk down the aisle, you fall off the back of the coach?"

"Of course not, silly," said Guinevere, "There's a seat at the end of the aisle …"

"Oh," she added.

"Exactly," said Merlin. "The single seat is at the back of the coach in the middle. There are two double seats at the front of the coach."

"I think I shall have to go back to the drawing board and rewrite it all," said Guinevere.

"Yes, I think your friend ought to," said Merlin smiling.

Note:

This chapter is based on a true incident mentioned in my history of our coach company, 'Memoirs of a Coach-Operating Man' (available on Amazon).

A customer became most argumentative and irate when she ordered a 29-seater coach from us and was not happy with the seat configuration, even though this was the standard layout for coaches (excluding those with reclining seats, toilets, et cetera).

For operational reasons, we sometimes sent out larger coaches than ordered (not smaller, of course), but in this instance it was a Bedford VAS coach with exactly 29 seats that we supplied, as she had requested.

As she had ordered a 29-seater and twenty-nine was an odd number, she clearly expected to occupy a single seat at the front, which, as organiser, she intended to have all to herself and not to have to share with her party.

When the driver pointed out respectfully that the single seat was, in fact, in the middle at the back of the coach, she became even more irate!

Whether she ever booked any more coaches from us, or whether she booked two seats for herself in future, I am afraid I can't remember.

Case 2023/011

The Woman Who Loved Fatty Arbuckle

Martin Walter phoned Merlin Protheroe early one Friday morning.

He seemed rather flustered.

"Look, I'm sure it's all right, but I can't find my wife. I don't know where she is. I was hoping your detective agency could find her, as the police seem to think it's too early to start worrying about her …"

Merlin agreed to call around as soon as he was available …

… Which was immediately, as he had no other work on his books, and had had none for some weeks.

-oOo-

Daffodil Cottage was clearly once a coach house at the bottom of the garden of a larger detached property overlooking the Severn Estuary. The "cottage" itself was narrow, but well enough designed to seem spacious.

Martin Walter opened the door, wringing his hands. He was a short man with a few strands of hair combed parallel on his head. He seemed a rather timid sort but was surprisingly sporting one of those aprons that feature the image of a scantily clad female figure.

"No news?" Merlin asked.

Martin Walter shook his head. "I'm afraid I've found a note now … a sort of, well, farewell note."

"I got in from work yesterday to find Megan not yet back from the cinema. She goes Thursday afternoons to a local hall where they show films. It may have been some film with Rock Hudson or Cary Grant … or one of those matinee idols anyway."

"Brad Pitt or Matt Damon, perhaps," volunteered Merlin.

"No, I don't know them. Anyway, I don't know what film it was. I don't like films particularly myself. But she's usually home by seven. I found this on the dining-room table."

"We bought it from IKEA," he added proudly.

He handed over a note: "Martin, I've been thinking a lot of late. I feel I've really had enough now, so I'm ending it all. Megan"

Merlin read it. It seemed like a typical suicide note. He remembered at one time that there were books that instructed one how to write perfect invitations, acceptance letters, business correspondence and other formal notes. Merlin wondered whether nowadays there was some webpage on the internet that gave advice on how to phrase suicide notes, as they were all so similar.

However, trying to be reassuring, he said, "It's rather short and perhaps a little vague. Does she mean she's going away for a while?"

Martin Walter shrugged.

Merlin took a photograph of the note Megan had left, and then suggested a chat over a cup of tea about Megan's usual haunts and friends and where she might have gone. Then he'd start a search and arrange for enquiries to be made. He tried to reassure his client that he was certain she'd turn up somewhere.

-oOo-

Megan Walter did turn up somewhere. Her body was found the next day, lying in a dry culvert a short distance away from her house and near some woods. Her body was so bent and twisted from the fall that she would have died instantly. The police doctor had averred that her injuries were consistent with such a fall.

Merlin made another visit to Martin Walter. He arrived early as he wanted to get there before the police. He wanted to avoid getting under their feet.

Merlin tried to sum things up, "I'm afraid it all looks as if your wife must have been suffering from some form of depression. The note confirms her intentions, and so any further investigation should merely be a formality."

"But do you have any examples of your wife's handwriting for comparison purposes? I'm sure the police would want something like that to close the case."

Martin Walter rummaged in a drawer in a sideboard and produced a few sheets of writing paper. "These were written when my wife went to hospital a few months ago, and I can't think of anything else she has written recently."

"Why did she have to go into hospital?" asked Merlin, wondering if the visit might have some bearing upon recent events.

"Oh, she had a small fall. It was nothing serious, er, physically, just bruises and suchlike. But they kept her in for a few days for observation. There was some suggestion that she might be suffering from dementia or something like that. But she seemed OK, so they let her come home."

He shrugged.

Merlin took a few photographs of the letters with his mobile phone.

Suddenly, there was an imperious rap on the door and the investigating officer announced his arrival. It was Detective Inspector Henry Medlar.

After Merlin had been introduced as "a friend," DI Medlar had looked quite suspiciously at him and tried to keep him out of the conversation. He gave his condolences, said the usual platitudes as he had been taught, and was then given the letters that Martin Walter had shown Merlin.

Having said all he felt he needed to say, DI Medlar returned to the station with the letters "for experts to compare the handwriting."

-oOo-

Merlin thought that the handwriting seemed a perfect match. The police agreed and prepared to close the case (Merlin was privy to information, in the vaguest sense, from his brother in the force).

But Merlin was still a little worried about the case. Having met Martin Walter, Merlin felt that there was something that just didn't seem quite right ...

He checked what had been showing at the local hall. He was surprised to find that, each afternoon, they had a film club, showing old Hollywood films of the silent era. For some weeks they had been showing a series of old Fatty Arbuckle shorts. Merlin discovered that Megan Walter had certainly visited the cinema that day, as she visited regularly and had been recognised. He wondered if she had a crush on Fatty Arbuckle.

He had to make one final visit to Daffodil Cottage as he wanted to clarify one small point. On the way, as he reported to his sister Guinevere, he happened to chance upon the postman, but, in truth, he had driven around the area for some time before he happened to "chance upon the postman."

Merlin stopped his car a few doors down from where the postman was delivering and waited for him. "Excuse me, but do you deliver to Daffodil Cottage?"

The postman hesitated and was reluctant to continue until he had been shown some form of identification by Merlin, not that the card he showed was really anything other than a confusingly crafted business card.

"Well, yes, that's part of my round."

"Do you ever deliver anything other than bills, anything personal that is, to the cottage?"

The postman nodded. "There's usually one personal letter a month, addressed to Mrs. Walter. The sender always puts her name and address on the back of the envelope, I assume in case I misdeliver the letter. I never do, of course."

"And the name and address?" asked Merlin, hopefully.

"It's a Miss Scantlebury in Bath. I can't quite remember the whole address, but I doubt there are many people called Scantlebury in Bath."

Merlin thanked the postman, and decided not to visit his client just yet.

-oOo-

It was indeed easy to determine the sender of the letters from Bath.

Miss Adeline Scantlebury was quite ancient, but in full possession of her faculties.

She was Megan Walter's aunt, whom she recently decided to try and trace after many years had elapsed after a family argument between Miss Scantlebury and Megan's mother.

They had begun corresponding.

And Miss Scantlebury had a few of Megan's letters to hand.

Merlin thought it would be worthwhile to make the drive to Bath to look at the letters and perhaps borrow a few.

The handwriting bore a resemblance to that in the farewell note … but was certainly not the same.

Merlin was sufficiently sure of what had actually happened to get in touch with his brother, DI Arthur Protheroe, and make him aware of his findings.

And experts decided that Megan Walter's handwriting and that on the farewell letter were different, although the latter was almost identical to Martin Walter's own handwriting.

Upon advice from Merlin's brother, DI Medlar obtained a search warrant, and traces were found of Megan Walter's blood by the fireplace in her house.

Faced with the evidence, Martin Walter confessed, "I become very jealous of Megan, after she started spending so much time away from me. I was certain the cinema visits were a cover for some less innocent pursuits, and that there was some man behind it all. I even tried following her on a number of occasions, but I'm not really cut out to be a detective, and she spotted me every time."

"So, in a rage, I must have pushed her a little too forcibly towards the fireplace. I was shocked when I realised she was actually dead. So I dumped her body in that culvert. I wanted to cover it all up, so I forged a suicide note, trying to copy my wife's handwriting from those letters she'd written. I suppose I didn't do it well enough ..."

He sounded quite pathetic.

Nevertheless, he was arrested and sentenced for his wife's murder.

Case 2023/012

The Route of All Evil

Barney Dawes was wandering back home from work along Cardiff Road, Barry, one evening at seven. He had recently been prescribed some new medication, and he now realised he would have to make a dash for some cover to relieve himself. He headed quickly down between two industrial units on the trading estate there … and discovered a body slumped between two parked cars. Barney forgot all about his urgency, much to his later chagrin.

-oOo-

The police were called, and Detective Inspector Arthur Protheroe found himself in charge of the case. The victim, who had been stabbed efficiently, was quickly identified.

Septimus Fitch was very, very rich, not a billionaire certainly, but he owned at least four or five houses … and he was always very vague about the number of properties he owned to suggest his insouciance about his wealth. He also owned a few companies he had purchased at knockdown prices when the original owners had got into financial difficulties.

He had paid for his two sons, Charles and Henry, to attend the very best university, but the two of them got together and reasoned that, if their father had that much money, then there was little need for them to work hard to get a degree. So they both left university and returned home to Barry.

However, they soon discovered that paying for them to go to a top university was the only thing their father was willing to pay for, and, despite almost constant pleas, they continued their lives, as their father said, "as penniless layabouts."

Charles managed to get a job as a bus driver based in Cardiff but serving also the Penarth and Barry areas. Henry just rested … he wasn't an actor, he just did nothing.

One of Septimus Fitch's businesses was a holding company based in a small unit at Cardiff Road Business Park on Cardiff Road, Barry, just on the Cardiff side of the Cadoxton railway bridge. Just what the company did, or even held, nobody seemed quite sure.

And it was near his office there that he had been found slumped between two parked cars. He had been stabbed, the doctor averred, that evening between four and seven, when his body was found. There was no sign of the knife. And it was hardly likely that he had been killed much earlier than six, as the whole area was quite busy up until that time, and his body was placed fairly prominently, certainly not hidden away.

As it seemed unlikely to be a random killing, there were only his two sons as suspects, as Mrs. Fitch, Septimus' wife, had divorced him many years previously and was now residing happily in Australia.

-oOo-

As DI Arthur Protheroe habitually did when he was getting nowhere with a case, he met up with his brother, Merlin, in the 'Blue Anchor' in East Aberthaw.

"I've only got two suspects, either of whom would seem capable of killing their father. There was certainly no love lost between any of them. Henry has no alibi, as he says he was at home on his own. But it looks as if his brother, Charles, has been set up to be the chief suspect. Either that, or he must be pretty stupid to make things so obvious."

Merlin nodded encouragement.

"That evening, Charles was driving a bus on a service from Wood Street, Cardiff, via Penarth and Sully, to the big Morrison's supermarket in Barry. And there's a bus stop on that route by Palmerston School. I assume you know where that is."

Merlin nodded. "It's more or less at the junction of Palmerston Road and Cardiff Road, about a third of a mile from Cardiff Road Business Park."

Now Arthur nodded. "Exactly, so that puts him a short distance from where Septimus Fitch was found dead. And we've checked, and he would have been driving a bus that was scheduled to stop at that bus stop at 1823, which would put Charles in the right area at the right time. So, did the murderer try to incriminate Charles, or is Charles not that bright … or is this some sort of double bluff?"

Merlin didn't nod this time. "In fact, what you've said rather gives Charles a good alibi, instead of suggesting he's your murderer."

Arthur looked a little blank.

"You see, Charles was driving a bus on a specified route, as authorised by the Traffic Commissioners. He certainly isn't supposed to leave the route for any reason except, I suppose, some sort of emergency. He could hardly deviate by around a third of a mile each way to commit a murder. So he could hardly have murdered his father, and perhaps the real murderer didn't realise that."

Arthur disagreed. "No, to me, Charles seems the more likely killer. So, what might he have done? The doctor said Septimus Fitch's body was almost certainly not moved. But Charles could have stopped the bus and run all the way to where his father was found. Or did he take the bus and any passengers on board with him? As it was an older bus, there was no CCTV fitted, but there certainly were passengers on board at every stage of the journey. And the transport company has received no comments or complaints from anyone, and there probably would have been a fair number of senior citizens on board, and you know how they like to complain … Anyone younger might not have noticed if they were absorbed in their iPods or whatever youngsters use these days."

Merlin thought, "And, in either case, the tachograph, the so-called "spy in the cab," probably wouldn't show anything unusual."

Arthur nodded. "You're right. And there were no records kept of who was on the bus at the relevant times. But there have been no complaints from passengers that they had been delayed whilst their driver committed patricide."

"So, that leaves me with the other son, Henry. He has no alibi whatsoever. But I have no evidence against him either. After all, there were no witnesses to the murder and nothing in the way of forensic evidence. Perhaps I should have a further talk with him and try and get some sort of confession out of him."

Merlin thought for a while. "Look, leave it with me for a day or two. I shall see what I can unearth."

Arthur nodded and reluctantly bought another round of drinks.

-oOo-

In the old days, Merlin would have had to have put an advert in the local press, as indeed Sherlock Holmes was often wont to do. There again, in Sherlock Holmes' days, any such advertisement would have been published within an hour or two of submission, and, as everyone read the papers in those days, any response would be received within the hour.

But now they had Facebook and other social media.

Merlin set up an entry in a few relevant sites on Facebook. He gave the date and the time, and then wrote,

"Would any passenger who travelled yesterday evening on the 94 bus from Cardiff to Barry, leaving Wood Street at 1740, and who witnessed anything unusual please reply to me via a DM."

Merlin was also a bit unsure how to phrase the entry. He had a fairly good idea what had happened, but felt he needed to be as vague as possible, as he wasn't quite sure exactly how things had been done. But he had to make sure that anyone reading it would respond.

And he had a response from two passengers on that particular departure.

Merlin got in touch with both respondents. Their descriptions of what had happened agreed completely. And both asked if "the lady" were OK now. They seemed to assume that the Facebook request had been put up in order to assist with some insurance claim on her behalf.

All this fitted in with most aspects of Merlin's theory.

One of the passengers who replied to Merlin's request for information, Harry Davies, said, "The driver announced that he was having problems with his visibility, and that he would have to adjust the mirror for safety reasons. He said he would have to pull off the road somewhere safe to make the adjustment, and so he didn't turn off Cardiff Road into Palmerston Road, where the next bus stop was, but continued on to some sort of trading estate to reposition the mirror. But it only took a few seconds, so, after he had turned the bus around at the next roundabout, he returned to Palmerston Road bus stop, and, as I think he had been running a little early anyway, I doubt that any people waiting at the subsequent bus stops would have registered anything amiss."

"But, when the driver got off the bus, we heard a shout, well, a scream actually. It seemed an old lady had fallen over and screamed out as she fell. All the passengers on board noticed, and one fairly elderly but fit gentleman went to help her. Then she seemed OK. Was this enquiry in regard to some insurance claim for her?"

Merlin assured him that the lady was fine, and thanked him for his help. He requested a description of the "old lady," which he was given.

And Henrietta MacHinery agreed with the story. Their descriptions of the lady tallied perfectly.

-oOo-

Merlin reported back to his brother with this new information, and Arthur carried out a few further investigations.

The two witnesses' descriptions of the "old lady" not only tallied with each other, but they also tallied with that of Charles' wife, Maura, who had ambitions of being an actress.

Charles had decided to murder his father for his inheritance.

He had arranged to meet his father at the trading estate and had then lied about having to adjust the bus's mirror and had driven off-route "somewhere safe." His wife, dressed as an old lady, had also been waiting there to put on an act of falling over, so that the passengers would have their attention drawn to that side of the bus, away from the side where Charles was "attending" discreetly to his father.

And all this cost Arthur a further round of drinks.

Note:

I wrote this story after it was "created / suggested" by one of these large language model-based chatbots. If you have never tried one, you have to enter key words, and it generates a new set of answers, replies, or even plot hints.

Apparently, it doesn't rely on a set of prepared answers or plots, but generates these uniquely, so, that, in my case, it can't result in any copyright problems or copycat accusations.

I tried it at the behest of my son-in-law in Norway, who, with my daughter, runs Snuti, which handles the annual summer reading programme for the Norwegian libraries, Sommerles.no.

However, I was largely unsuccessful in getting ideas or plots from the chatbot. It tended to be very vague (along the lines of "A man is murdered but the case is solved using a very clever plot twist" (!)), although it was quite good at coming up with background motives. It also often suggested supernatural or alien intervention as the solution. The only possibly useful plot I obtained I based this story on. Perhaps it "kind of" works, but it took a lot of reworking and fiddling to wrap it into a full short story, and to try and make it a little cohesive.

And I am not too sure I've succeeded.

Case 2023/013

Following Up a Lead

"My darling little Perdita has vanished!" wailed Dolly Lovell.

Perdita was clearly a dog. Merlin Protheroe tried to decide whether Mrs. Lovell was a devotee of Shakespeare or of Dodie Smith and Walt Disney, but then looked again at Mrs. Lovell and decided it was definitely the latter.

He had the same attitude towards accepting cases of missing dogs as funeral directors no doubt have towards being asked to arrange pet funerals, but, well, he was a little short of work, and, more importantly, money at the moment …

"Do tell me what happened," he said solicitously, although he knew full well she would anyway.

"Well, my husband took my darling little Perdita, she's a sweet little Cavalier King Charles Spaniel, out for her usual walk just after six. He always takes the same path, because he's a creature of habit, and so is Perdita. He always takes her from our house in Sully, along the footpath opposite the church down to the coastal path, and then along the path towards Barry for as long as she wants ... or actually until she does her business."

Merlin knew the walk well, as he had taken a large number of rambles around the area whilst being unable to travel farther due to the constraints imposed during the COVID-19 outbreak.

"And she hasn't come home?" asked Merlin unnecessarily.

Dolly Lovell shook her head and filled a large handkerchief she had been twisting in her hands.

"And what does your husband say happened?" asked Merlin.

Again, she shook her head.

"He hasn't come home either."

Merlin was rather taken aback with the way the conversation had gone and said nothing for about thirty seconds.

Then he continued, "Well, I have a few contacts in the canine world around here, so I shall do some checking and then get back to you."

Merlin took down a description of Mr. Lovell, and, although no photographs of him were available, he was showered profusely with photographs of Perdita.

"But, if your husband doesn't return home soon, I would get in touch with the police."

"Oh, but I already have done, but they said they're not interested in looking for lost dogs. They're so unfeeling."

-oOo-

Having ascertained that nobody answering Mr. Lovell's description had been admitted to hospital in the last twenty-four hours, Merlin started his search. He took the walk that Perdita and Mr. Lovell had taken. He suddenly realised that Mrs. Lovell had neglected to tell him her husband's first name ...

It was a pleasant enough walk. Sully Church is one of the many Norman and mediaeval churches in the Vale of Glamorgan. A footpath leads from almost opposite the church down to the local section of the Wales Coast Path, which follows as closely as possible the coastline of Wales for 870 miles and was the first dedicated coast path in the world to cover the entire length of a country's coastline. From that point, Merlin turned to the west, the way that Mrs. Lovell said her husband would have taken. The coast path leads past a large field; a public car park by the lane that runs from Hayes Road past the old recycling centre; a children's hospice, Tŷ Hafan, where are still some of the Snowdog sculptures that had been displayed around Cardiff in 2017 to raise money for the Hospice; past the splendid Art Deco building that was once Sully Hospital; and on to the Bendricks, where dinosaur footprints can be seen on the rocky shore.

But Merlin ignored the coast path itself when walking west, as his initial interest was in checking the shore for traces of the missing dog and Mr. Lovell. He wondered whether perhaps they had fallen onto the rocks here. It was not a great drop, but the shore was very rocky. But he could find nothing.

As he prepared to return along the path itself, Merlin started considering what the likely possibilities were.

Mr. Lovell was unlikely to have taken a different route, as Mrs. Lovell said he always took the same path.

Had he decided to run away? Having met Mrs. Lovell, Merlin could fully understand such an action.

And Merlin doubted that Mr. Lovell would have had the nerve to kidnap Perdita and hold her to ransom (again, because he had met Mrs. Lovell).

Merlin could only assume that someone had attacked or kidnapped Mr. Lovell or Perdita and had taken them away.

But, in that case, they would surely have had to have been taken away by car or van, as there seemed to be no private properties alongside the path. And the pathway was very public, so the vehicle would have had to have been parked nearby to minimise the chance of the incident being seen by anybody.

And the only place that was convenient was the public car park in the lane near the old Hayes Road recycling centre.

Merlin retraced his steps along the pathway. This time he examined the grass and hedge on either side of the path.

And finally he found something.

There was a small patch of grass where some blood was in evidence. Whether it was that of a dog or a human, Merlin wasn't sure. But it was where Merlin had surmised the incident, whatever it was, would have had happened, near to the public car park.

He checked, but there seemed to be no CCTV cameras in the car park, not that he would have expected that.

Then he saw an elderly couple approaching with a small corgi on a lead.

Merlin decided it was time to lie.

"Excuse me, but I'm looking for my dog. He escaped. Are there any dangerous or out-of-control dogs around here who might have frightened or attacked him?"

The elderly couple looked at one another. It was the woman who answered.

"Well, I don't like to point the finger, as it were, but there's one of those XXL American Bully dogs that's often exercised along here. We changed the time we come to visit because of its aggressive attitude towards other dogs, even large ones, so our little Berenice would stand no chance against him. Its owners just don't see to be able to control it, nor, for that matter, to care."

Merlin noted down a description of the owners and their dog, and then contacted a friend of his who adored dogs and who lived in the area.

Soon he had an address.

It was only a theory he had, but he felt it was worth investigating ...

He parked his car a little farther down the lane from the address he had been given and wandered over. The lane led out into the countryside from Sully and would probably dwindle out eventually in some farmyard. There were a few houses around, but not many.

The house was a small end-of-terrace house with a shed built from breeze blocks in the garden. There were also a few small hutches, as if the owner had ambitions to being a farmer.

Merlin felt it was probably safe to investigate a little further, as there was no car in the drive and no garage, and anyone living out here would have to own a vehicle out of necessity. He was also encouraged by the lack of barking coming from inside the house, as he knew that a XXL American Bully dog lived here.

Merlin rattled the door of the shed, and was rewarded by the sound of barking, although very faint, coming from inside ... and most certainly not the noises one would expect from a large dog such as the XXL American Bully

Merlin was pondering what to do next when he heard the sound of a vehicle approaching.

He was thinking of vaulting (or, at his age, clambering) over the clearly unstable wall at the back of the property when he decided that, as time was of the essence, it was advisable to be more direct (or, as Guinevere later put it, "foolhardy").

As the driver got out of the ancient Land Rover (and, Merlin reasoned, before he had time to open the back to let the dog out), Merlin wandered casually up to him.

"I'm looking for a Mr. Lovell and his dog. Do you know where they might be?"

The driver looked a rough sort, and Merlin was beginning to think he had made the wrong decision and was waiting to be unceremoniously bundled into the house, or worse.

The driver was quickly joined by his wife, but, thankfully, not the dog, which was making its presence uncomfortably felt from the back of the Land Rover. But, to Merlin's surprise, they seemed happy to talk.

Harry Dobbins and his wife Lavinia admitted that their dog, Gnasher, had indeed attacked Perdita, but Mr. Lovell had, as they put it, "gone ballistic," threatening them with the police, jail, and even a visit from his wife, so they hid both him and his dog in their house whilst they considered their options, and had that afternoon gone to a friend to seek advice. In fact, they would have been quite happy to release both man and dog, if it weren't for Mr. Lovell's "unreasonable threats and vindictiveness," as they put it.

Perdita made a full recovery, although Merlin wasn't completely convinced that Mr. Lovell would, after he told Merlin of the sort of reception he would receive from his wife.

But Mr. Lovell's actions and attitude towards Harry and Lavinia Dobbins did seem totally alien to his usual personality. He wondered whether in fact Mr. Lovell was just terrified of admitting to his wife his part in what had happened.

Merlin knew he would have been.

Case 2023/014

Honeymoon Sweet

The Hotel 'Bien Marié' specialised in wedding receptions and corporate events.

It had been created from a large impressive stately home that nobody could afford to run as a private property, although somebody suggested perhaps it could be sympathetically changed into a Tesco Extra Extra supermarket. This idea was soon quashed when it was pointed out that the nearest village was over fifteen miles away. And workhouses were so out-of-fashion these days. Even asylum-seekers baulked at staying there as the nearest shop was in the aforementioned village fully fifteen miles away.

So it had become an hotel, a rather impressive one.

The only thing that was not so impressive was that the electricians and signwriters had decided that their patron could not spell and had consulted a dictionary before erecting the huge illuminated sign at the entrance. It proudly proclaimed 'Hotel Bain-Marie.'

The co-owner of the hotel, Mario Rossi (born Martin Ross), intended to get the sign fixed as soon as the money was available, which, the way things were looking, was not likely to be very soon.

He had had high hopes of making a financial killing with a society wedding this weekend, as the building had been booked for a wedding reception for one of the Harcourt family, rich and prominent local landowners. But the groom, Grant Harcourt, was not part of the wealthy side of the family, and few of the hotel's vast array of rooms had been booked. The remaining members of the party had baulked at the prices, and had decided to decamp to the TravelShed, fifteen miles away.

In fact, the groom was one of old Sir Henry Harcourt's three sons, but he had been disinherited when he had upset his father greatly. Firstly, he had insisted on marrying beneath his station when he announced his engagement to Jade O'Sullivan, a bit-part actress, celebrity (although by which definition nobody seemed sure) and influencer. Secondly, he had spent a few months in jail after a "misunderstanding," as Grant himself had termed it. And, thirdly - and most importantly - he had refused to take part in the local hunt, of which his father was the local Master of Foxhounds.

Mario thought the reception had gone well. Much money had been spent at the bar. Nobody had been ill. "What more could one ask for?" Mario thought.

Mario had checked that the rooms were ready, well-aired, and that, in the Honeymoon Suite, "that smell" had finally gone away.

The wedded couple, Grant and Jade Harcourt had gone to bed early. This had surprised the guests as neither had clearly been keeping themselves for this night. The guests themselves kept the bar running until the consumption slowed down sufficiently for Mario to decide that the overtime outweighed the profits and that the bar should close in ten minutes. That, he was pleased to note, at least stirred up sales for those ten minutes.

Then everybody went to bed. Those in the rooms adjoining the Honeymoon Suite had expected perhaps to have to endure a fairly noisy night, but even they were stunned at the loud screams that came from the room around one o'clock. Had Grant been a little too experimental or had Jade misunderstood his intentions?

In fact, it was neither.

Tearfully, Jade rushed out onto the landing. "My Grant, he's dead. Someone's killed him."

The guests in the nearest room thought that perhaps Grant had merely become a little over-exhausted, so they checked.

But he was indeed deceased.

-oOo-

Merlin Protheroe arrived at the hotel at almost exactly the same time as his brother, Detective Inspector

Arthur Protheroe, who was accompanied by PC Watkins. They had arrived just as soon as they could find the place. The official car's sat nav had packed up and PC Watkins's map-reading skills were largely non-existent. He had described trying to locate the huge mansion in the middle of a large tract of open land as like "finding a needle in a haystack."

"So, what are you doing here?" DI Protheroe asked his brother.

"Well, the hotel was hoping that I might be able to solve the case quickly, before there was any adverse publicity, but, as there was a suspicious death involved, I told them they would have to contact your outfit as well."

DI Protheroe wasn't sure about the local constabulary being referred to as an "outfit," but nodded happily. He always liked to have as much help on hand as he could.

"Welcome, welcome," enthused Mario Rossi. "I do hope we can clear this up quickly and, er, cleanly."

All three were led into the Honeymoon Suite, where the doctor was just finishing his examination.

"Simple enough. It couldn't be food poisoning from the wedding dinner, as everyone had the same meal, prawn cocktail, roast chicken and fresh garden vegetables, and Black Forest gateau. Everyone else is fine, although, with a menu like that, I imagine they all felt they'd spent the evening in some sort of 1960s time warp."

"No, the culprit is there." He pointed to the pillow.

"Smothered?" asked Merlin.

"No, they do that daft thing of putting a chocolate on the pillow for each guest."

Merlin hated the idea too. A friend of his had turned up in his hotel room a little drunk, hadn't noticed the chocolate on the pillow, and had slept on it. He had woken up thinking he'd haemorrhaged in the night.

Merlin asked, "So, why did only the groom die? Did his wife not like chocolates?"

The doctor shook his head. "She's female, so of course she liked chocolates. But that's the odd thing. Only one chocolate was poisoned."

Merlin frowned.

"It was a fairly simple little poison. I'm sure there's some in the kitchen or the outhouse somewhere here. So either some guest brought the poison with them, or they sought it out below stairs. That's your job to find out, I suppose."

DI Protheroe went in search of Jade Harcourt. He frequently found that the wives of husbands who had just been murdered were often quite composed.

Often it seemed they were rather satisfied, even pleased, with the outcome.

Not in this case, of course. The recently married and even-more-recently bereaved wife was hysterical, to put it very mildly. DI Protheroe doubted that she was sufficiently proficient at acting to achieve the state she was in.

All he could get out of her was that the chocolates looked identical, there being no difference in their wrapping, and that they had had a free choice which to eat.

-oOo-

DI Protheroe and Merlin were confused.

Assuming that the murderer was not Jade Harcourt herself, why had the killer only poisoned one chocolate? Had he or she forgotten to treat the second chocolate ... or had mistakenly put a double dose in one ... or just didn't care ... or what?

And who had a motive?

Mario Rossi certainly didn't, as he would be finding it even more difficult now to fill the hotel or even to sell it.

As it was, there were few guests in the hotel, in fact, only those who were attending the reception and who could afford to stay the night. And this amounted to only five couples, mainly because members of the richest side of the family had all consigned their invitations to the wastepaper bin, and the less well-off guests had elected to stay at a cheaper hotel some way away.

As the hotel had an excellent security system, there were no outsiders who might be considered, and there were only three members of staff who stayed overnight.

"Only three members of staff?" DI Protheroe had asked Rossi.

"Look, we're on our uppers. The old man and the girls can cope with the bar and room preparation when the hotel isn't too full, and it certainly isn't this weekend … and I'm always available if need be."

DI Protheroe decided to interview the staff members first, as one of these would presumably have the responsibility for the ritualistic placing of chocolates on the pillows.

As with many impecunious hotels, staff members had a range of responsibilities each. The rooms were cleaned and prepared by Debbie Daniels and Katy Wright. But it was the former who had prepared the Honeymoon Suite.

"Katy did the other rooms, but I was assigned just to the Honeymoon Suite, as it was larger, and it was most important that it be clean and impressive. And yes, I put the chocolates on the pillow. But I just took them at random out of a box from stock. They were supplied by Shellard and Phideau. That's a top brand."

DI Protheroe nodded. He had heard of them but couldn't justify the cost of buying that brand.

"Katy had the box first as she had the other rooms to do. When she'd finished, she gave me the box. I put the chocolates on the pillow at ten. I know it was ten, because I checked my watch, as I thought it must be time to go back below stairs for my hot chocolate. And then, later, I returned the box to the kitchen store."

"And could anyone else have had access to the box of chocolates?" asked DI Protheroe.

"If they knew where it was, but there's an awful lot of stuff in the kitchen."

Neither chambermaid, or whatever they were called these days, could add anything more.

Apart from Mario Rossi, the only other member of staff on duty that night was Harry Raybould, who manned the front desk (although the hotel was effectively locked up for the night after ten-thirty), organised room service if required, and acted as security (although DI Protheroe wondered what such an old man could do if challenged by anyone else, unless they were severely disabled).

Harry had been at the front desk from ten until the time he was alerted, or perhaps woken, by the scream. Then he had busied himself helping out and dialling 999.

Neither she nor the chambermaids appeared to have any motive for the murder.

All the time that DI Protheroe had been interviewing the staff, Mario Rossi had been hovering alongside. When he himself was interviewed he also had little to say. He had been in attendance during the evening but had retired to his room as soon as the bar had closed and the money had been securely locked up. He had not been woken up by the screams but had been roused from his slumbers by Harry Raybould. He also admitted that there was some poison kept on the premises, but in an outhouse. The gardener apparently had to keep certain pests under control. When pressed he also admitted that the outhouse was in fact the garage, and so perhaps the guests had seen that when parking. He winced.

DI Protheroe then interviewed the five couples, the Walters, the Johnsons, the Stanley-Normans, the Cains, and some Harcourts, distant members of the family who hadn't really known about the disinheritance.

All the younger guests had left the hotel at nine-forty-five, well before the deadly chocolates had been placed on the pillow. Half of them admitted that they had been unable to afford the high prices charged by the wedding hotel, and the others just said that they had had no wish to stay there with a "load of old fogeys," and so had decided to stay in the TravelShed.

All those who remained in the hotel had said about the same, that they had all been in the bar until the (then) happy couple had left around ten-thirty and had then found that they didn't really have much in common with the other wedding guests. So, as they felt they had drunk enough already, they all wandered off to their respective bedrooms around eleven. Those nearest the Honeymoon Suite had heard the screams that began at one o'clock, and Mrs. Cain had been the first on the scene, as she and her husband occupied the nearest room.

-oOo-

"So, where are we, Merlin?" asked DI Protheroe disconsolately. "We have few suspects and no motive. All the younger guests were out of the hotel by the time the chocolates had been placed on the pillow, and I can't see any motive that the older guests might have had."

Merlin nodded in agreement.

"Having talked to the guests who stayed at the hotel overnight, I felt none of them seemed very close to the bride or groom, but just seemed to be the sort of family relatives that one feels one must invite to a wedding. I was wondering whether the murder might have been a result of someone feeling jilted, shall we say, but that could hardly apply to such old folk."

"And you've checked that every one of the guests staying at the hotel is indeed rich enough to easily pay for their accommodation without it embarrassing them financially, so it's not a case of someone staying purely to be able to administer the coup de grâce."

"And none of the younger ones had time to poison the chocolate before leaving."

"Or should we dig deeply into the backgrounds of all our suspects in case one of the older ones is related to someone who has been hurt by our bride or groom?"

"And did our murderer smuggle in the poison, as part of a premeditated crime? We've searched everyone and everywhere and the only poison is in the garage, although anybody who knew where it was could have had access to it."

"But there's one thing that I really cannot understand. Why would anybody poison one of a pair of chocolates, not knowing which of the two occupants of the room would eat the poisoned one?"

Merlin stopped talking and thought for a while.

"I can think of one good reason why only one chocolate was poisoned ... provided we assume that killer wasn't forgetful or incompetent or suffering from dementia."

"And so I think we need to interview quite a few of our suspects … but there are two I'd like to start with. You'd better ask PC Watkins to get the car."

-oOo-

And Merlin got lucky with the first of the two he particularly wanted to interview.

Mrs. Mary Bridgeman lived on her own in a converted barn a few miles away.

"Well, I've remarried a few times, but I'm still here on my own." She smiled benignly.

"And I gather Katy was your daughter from a previous marriage," said Merlin.

"Yes. She's a lovely girl. She works at the Hotel Bain-Marie, or something like that."

"And has she ever been, shall we say, upset in a relationship?"

Mrs. Bridgeman looked a little askance, as if she didn't really want to answer the question. Then she clearly remembered that this was a police investigation, and continued, "Well, Katy was always such a naive girl, always falling in love with the wrong person. Then at last she seemed to have got it right. She got engaged to that Grant Harcourt, from what we thought was one of the richest families in the area. But it wasn't the money she was after. She really loved him."

"Anyway, he left her a few weeks before the wedding that she'd arranged and paid for. I think she's still paying off the debt."

-oOo-

It was as Merlin had suspected. Someone had poisoned the chocolate to get revenge for some previous misdemeanour. And, if his theory were correct, the fact that only one chocolate had been poisoned suggested that it was some romance that had gone badly awry, for one of the partners at least.

And the two most likely suspects were the two chambermaids. Although Merlin realised that DI Protheroe would perhaps have to interview the more elderly suspects in case the murder had been because of a younger relative who had been wronged, they had been lucky enough to choose the right person to interview first.

Forensics would probably come up with DNA or fingerprint evidence from the chocolate wrappings, but that wouldn't be absolutely necessary because Katy Wright seemed happy to confess when DI Protheroe said they knew everything.

She had waited until Debbie Daniels had finished the Honeymoon Suite and had then switched one chocolate for one she had previously put poison in.

She didn't seem particularly remorseful.

-oOo-

Merlin, his sister, Guinevere, and DI Protheroe were all sitting together in Merlin's favourite pub, the 'Blue Anchor' in East Aberthaw.

DI Protheroe looked perplexed. "But how did Miss Wright know that Grant Harcourt would eat the poisoned chocolate, and not the other one?"

Merlin smiled, "She didn't mind who ate the chocolate. If it were Grant, she'd have her revenge for his jilting her almost at the altar. If it were Jade, then she'd feel she was saving her from a disastrous marriage, as well as causing the same sort of grief to Grant that he had caused her."

DI Protheroe nodded. "Yes, that's the way I figured it out."

Although he hadn't.

All three were silent for a minute or two and then Guinevere added, sotto voce, "Perhaps she knew on which side of the bed Grant slept ..."

Case 2023/015

If You Go Down to the Woods Today …

"They've found a man with one arm hanging from a tree in Cwm George," announced Detective Inspector Arthur Protheroe.

DI Henry Medlar looked unimpressed. "So what? I can easily hang from a tree with one arm." He seemed serious.

It was only a short drive to Cwm George, and PC Watkins was on hand to direct DI Protheroe to the body. He had already done so for the doctor and the forensics team.

Wayne French had now been cut down and he was lying on the grass under the tree.

DI Protheroe had a quick word with the doctor, and then returned to PC Watkins, thinking aloud. "The doctor says that the time of death would be after one this afternoon, and he was found at four p.m. by a jogger. It's a fairly busy path through the woods, I suppose. But, as he only has the one arm, there's no way he could have climbed up that tree without something to stand on … and there are no suitable boxes or steps from which he could have launched himself. So, was it murder?"

PC Watkins was acting a little excitedly. "Or was he trying to make it look like murder? I have a theory …"

DI Protheroe sighed.

"I reckon he carried a huge block of ice up here, stood on it, and waited for it to melt, thus killing himself and making it look as if someone had murdered him. Voila!"

DI Protheroe sighed again. "Firstly, how would he carry a huge block of ice here when he only had one arm? I don't see any trolleys or anything similar around, although I concede he might have dumped the ice, and then hidden the trolley elsewhere."

"But secondly, the weather's been dry for months and it is rather cold. If Mr. French had stood on a block of ice, don't you think there might be some water around, or at least a little dampness in the ground?"

PC Watkins clicked his tongue irritably but said nothing.

The cause of death was obvious, and there was little enough forensic evidence around as the ground was so hard (which upset PC Watkins as it clearly frustrated his passionately held theory).

"We'll check on his background and see if he has any family," said DI Protheroe.

-oOo-

Wayne's only relative was his elderly mother.

She was naturally distraught, but she said she was composed enough to talk to DI Protheroe.

"Wayne led a very quiet life. He had few friends, hardly any, in fact. He lived just for his model-making, but the accident made that almost impossible for him."

She insisted on taking DI Protheroe into the spare room, where a large number of model aeroplanes were suspended from the ceiling. Model cars and tanks littered the various shelves strewn around the room. The models were not very well constructed and appeared to have been painted by someone returning from a long evening at the local pub.

"And Wayne made all these after his accident?" asked DI Protheroe, rather impressed.

"Oh no, he made these when he was still fit." Wayne's mother beamed proudly.

"So, what accident was your son involved in?"

"Oh, it was the usual drunk driver, although he said he was so shocked that he had to have a nip of whisky after the accident, and so the breathalyser test wasn't ruled admissible. The odd thing is that at least it gave

Wayne something to aim for in his life, a sort of purpose."

DI Protheroe smiled encouragingly.

"Well, Wayne could hardly continue with his hobby, but he felt he should try and bring the driver, Jason Porsche, to justice. He did a lot of research and found out that Jason was actually born as John Porch, but he clearly felt his new name more befitting his perceived status in life, although he only drove an elderly BMW."

"Anyway, I thought some of Wayne's actions were occasionally a little too intimidating, but he said that that's what Jason deserved. He used to phone Jason up at odd times, anonymously of course, and accuse him of causing the accident and other crimes. He would file complaints against him at work. Jason works as a sales executive at McQuay Windows, but Wayne reckoned he was only a general dogsbody."

"Do you think that Jason Porsche knew your son was behind all these complaints?" asked DI Protheroe.

"Well, I don't think he had any proof, but he must have suspected …" mused Mrs. French.

The only thing of interest was that Mrs. French said her son had left the house at two that afternoon. The house was only a short distance from Cwm George, so that narrowed down the time of death a little.

-oOo-

McQuay Windows occupied a large cluster of Portakabins on what appeared to be the site of an old brickworks.

Jason Porsche Sales Executive, as his name badge proclaimed, seemed rather a shifty individual, certainly not someone who either DI Protheroe would want to deal with in regard to having new windows installed.

"Yesterday? Well, that was a strange one. I had a phone call in the morning asking me to go to visit one of our clients, Hollywood Garden Sheds …"

DI Protheroe registered the fact that this garden centre was fairly near Cwm George.

"We had installed a few large windows for them a few months back, and they said there was a major fault with them. They were good customers, so I didn't try to fob them off, but arranged to see them, as they suggested, yesterday at two in the afternoon."

"Well, I always have lunch at a little roadside shack near here, but yesterday I noticed a new van that had parked much nearer. It was selling Indian food, which I adore, so I decided to eat there instead."

"Well, I wish I hadn't, as I had the most dreadful stomach problems. I just couldn't leave the office and go visiting anybody, so I phoned up Hollywood

Garden Sheds and asked them to change the appointment, but they said they hadn't actually contacted me at all. They said they were perfectly, well fairly, happy with the windows we had installed."

"So, I spent the whole afternoon on the phone in the office, near to the toilets. And my boss is a bit of a stickler, so I couldn't leave until six. Sue or Derek can vouch for me in that respect."

Two office workers, clearly Sue and Derek, had obviously been eavesdropping, and they both looked at DI Protheroe and nodded their agreement.

So, DI Protheroe had one body and one suspect … and he had a perfect alibi, it seemed. Perhaps it was suicide …

-oOo-

The 'Blue Anchor' is a charming little thatched pub in East Aberthaw in the Vale of Glamorgan. It was built in 1380. It was a favourite of his brother, Merlin, so DI Protheroe knew he would be happy to accompany him there for a drink and perhaps a light meal … even if he knew he was going to be consulted about a case with no remuneration involved.

DI Protheroe went over the details of the death of Wayne French.

His brother nodded sagely, but perhaps a little vacantly, and arranged to view the scene of the crime the next day.

DI Protheroe sighed. Yes, this was going to cost him a meal in the pub.

-oOo-

The following day, DI Protheroe picked up his brother to return to Cwm George.

However, en route, Merlin insisted on calling on Mrs. French.

DI Protheroe insisted that the visit was unnecessary. "I can assure you that I asked Mrs. French everything I needed to."

Merlin nodded. "I'm sure you have. But this won't take long."

Mrs. French was also surprised at the need for another chat and was even more surprised at Merlin's only question. "Er, did your son ever own a dog?"

She shook her head, clearly more than a little perturbed at the need for such a question.

The Protheroes continued on to Cwm George.

With the body and the police presence no longer there, the woods had returned to its usual bucolic atmosphere.

"What are we looking for?" asked DI Protheroe.

"I'm not sure. I'll know it when I see it … maybe," replied Merlin evasively.

He spent some time looking around in the undergrowth. He found some flattened flora, well away from where the forensics people might have trampled it. It looked as if something might have been dragged across the ground.

Merlin now had a theory, so, in order to try and prove it, he put up a message on Facebook, on a site helping owners to find their lost dogs and other pets. He said that he was trying to trace his dog, which had escaped, dragging away what it was it had been secured to.

And he had a number of replies.

Most of them castigated him for being careless and potentially hurting his pet. But a few pointed him in the direction of a local dog lover who took in strays and lost dogs and tried to return them to their rightful owners, using a dedicated site on Facebook. Merlin was surprised how often dog owners lost their pets, but the service seemed to work well, given the dedication of its organiser, Mrs. Marjorie Page.

A fairly large terrier, temporarily called Teddy, had been found wandering around, clearly lost and rather distressed, dragging a plastic chair behind him. Soon its owner had turned up to claim him, and it took a great deal of effort on Merlin's part to explain the situation and to stop Mrs. Page from berating him about the poor dog's sufferings.

The local pet network, working via Facebook, had managed to discover that the dog had been seen being carried off by a man with one arm …

Luckily, Mrs. Page still had the chair … which was covered in Wayne French's fingerprints.

DI Protheroe felt he had enough proof from Merlin that Wayne, having been unsuccessful in bringing Jason Porsche properly to justice, had decided to end it all and to suggest that Jason had murdered him because of his persistence. He had made an appointment for the window salesman to visit the garden centre very near to Cwm George at the appropriate time, and it was lucky for Jason that he had been unable to keep the appointment. Wayne had stolen a dog, tied it to a plastic chair he owned, and then probably thrown a stone at the dog to frighten it into running away, dragging the chair behind him.

DI Protheroe later explained to PC Watkins what had actually happened.

He though deeply for a while and then ventured, "But the ground below the body did look a little wet, Sir."

Case 2023/016

Post Bellum

"Are you Merlin Protheroe, PI?" asked Agatha Borysiewicz.

Merlin nodded, although his name was printed on the office door clearly enough.

"I've received a number of what I think are called poison pen letters," she said, "And I want to know who's sending them."

She handed one over.

It read:

"I know your having an affair with your neighbour, Mrs. Borysiewicz."

"And, before you ask, I'm not. It's just a friendly non-sexual relationship."

Merlin wasn't too surprised that it was non-sexual, as Mrs. Borysiewicz must have been nudging eighty, although, at that age, nudging is about all one can expect.

"And, anyway, it hardly matters, as my husband was buried last December."

Merlin nodded, but he wasn't sure exactly why.

He looked again at the letter. Each word had been cut in its entirety from another source. He recognised the typeface for almost all the words as being from the Penarth Equitable, a free local newspaper. That was presumably why 'your' had been misspelt, as that must have been the only word available that sounded like 'you're.' Or perhaps the sender of the letter was none too bright, as another element of the letter suggested.

"Perhaps you'd tell me a little about the background of your family," Merlin suggested.

Mrs. Borysiewicz looked a little surprised at the question. As Merlin's clients often did, she clearly just expected to provide a bit of evidence and then leave it to him to sort it all out.

"Well, I don't see what that has got to do with all this. I only wanted you to look at the letter and find out who's sending them. But anyway, I don't have any secrets. I was born here in Penarth in …" she gave a year that Merlin knew was a lie "… and I married my husband, Aleksander Borysiewicz, in Penarth in 1986. His father had arrived here after the war. But, as I said, he died last December."

"Any children?" asked Merlin.

"Well, I have one son, who, I'm ashamed to say, had a few scrapes with the law, drugs and that sort of thing, although I've always felt he was more of a victim. He now lives in Stevenage. But he was a bit of a tearaway, like my husband I suppose, as I later discovered. He had a mistress, someone else's wife."

Merlin thought that there seemed to be plenty of suspects here.

"Were there many people at the funeral?" asked Merlin.

"Why does that matter?" asked Mrs. Borysiewicz, irritably.

"I can assure you that it might," replied Merlin.

"About six people. He wasn't well-liked. Anyway, I'm not sure I liked him much when I found out about his affair."

Merlin continued, "The reason I ask is that each word in the letter you received was cut in its entirety from a source I recognise, the Penarth Equitable newspaper ... except one. And even that exception, your surname, is cut out as one word, although from a different source. Now, normally in a blackmail or poison pen letter any unusual words, such as your surname, would have been made up of individual letters, perhaps from the same source, but not in this case. Now, where would your surname have been printed?"

"Well, nowhere, of course," replied Mrs. Borysiewicz, even more irritably. "I don't publish books or write to the local newspaper."

"So, the probable source is the cards they distributed at the funeral …" suggested Merlin.

Mrs. Borysiewicz thought for a while, and then said, "Oh yes, of course."

"So, if we have a list of those who attended the funeral and another of those who might have a grudge against you or your husband or the members of your family, we can apply a sort of Venn diagram to see which names are on both lists."

"Yes!" screamed Mrs. Borysiewicz, "That's it! I remember now. The vicar's name was Venn! I never liked him. So you think he sent the letters?"

Merlin tried to calm her down. "No, no, that's not what I meant. We just have to compile a list of those who fit into both the two groups, those who attended the funeral and those with a grudge against your family."

Mrs. Borysiewicz agreed, and said, "At home I still have the box of funeral cards we bought from the printers. We had to pay for a minimum of fifty, so there were a lot unused, and I know there were only six which were given out."

So the compiling of the two lists was fairly easy.

And there was a clear result.

The only name on both the lists was Mrs. Borysiewicz's brother-in-law.

"He's always wanted me as a companion," muttered Mrs. Borysiewicz. "He keeps asking me out, especially since Aleksander's death. But I always turn him down. He always smells of chip fat."

"I shall go and have a word with him," said Merlin. He took down the address.

Mrs. Borysiewicz left the office. Merlin was surprised how fast she was able to move at her age.

Merlin was about to leave the office himself, to visit the brother-in-law, when the phone rang. It was an important client, well, the only other one at that particular moment in time, so he had to take the call. It turned out to be lengthier than he expected.

When Merlin finally got around to visiting the brother-in-law's terraced house in Salop Street, he was just in time to see Mrs. Borysiewicz leaving, slamming the front door as loudly as she could. She was in less of a hurry now. She beamed at Merlin. "I gave him hell, the little sod. Anyway, I made him confess."

She waltzed off like a teenager.

The door opened slowly and the brother-in-law, looking shocked and bemused, put his head around the door, and asked "Has she gone?"

Merlin nodded.

He only wished he and his brother were allowed to use such tactics in securing a confession.

Case 2023/017

How Long Would it Take the Police to Find Dead Bodies if it Weren't for Early-morning Dog Walkers?

"Sorry, Debbie," apologised Howard Jones, as he accidentally threw Debbie's favourite stick too high, and it landed in the lower branches of an ailing elm tree.

Debbie had originally been christened Joan (although, on the only occasion Debbie had actually been inside a church, she had disgraced herself by the font). She had been named after Howard's wife, but, after she had left him for a Turkish waiter, he renamed his dog after the pretty girl who worked behind the bar in the 'Coach and Lettuce.'

Having decided that he was really far too old to try climbing trees at his age, Howard was just grubbing around in the undergrowth looking for a replacement stick when Debbie returned with a much thicker, heavier stick in her mouth. Howard was surprised she was able to carry it.

Then he saw that it had a lot of blood on one end.

It took him a while to decide whether or not to tell the police about the blood. It might very well be of no importance whatsoever, and Howard hated making a fuss unnecessarily. But he finally resolved to phone the police the minute he got back to his car, which he had parked in a small unofficial lay-by on the edge of Leckwith Woods. He would have phoned there and then, but his spectacles were in the car.

But he didn't phone the police the minute he arrived back at his car. Debbie started sniffing around at the far end of the lay-by and barking, and so Howard went to look at the place where she was standing. Even without his glasses he could see a person slumped at the edge of the lay-by. The person was clearly dead.

A wound on the person's head seemed to match the end of the bloodied stick Debbie had retrieved, but Howard resisted the temptation to place the stick against the wound to see how closely it matched.

Howard finally phoned 999, and DI Protheroe and PC Watkins arrived about forty minutes later.

-oOo-

It was indeed a heavy stick, and so the cause of death initially seemed obvious. However, a further wound on the other side of the victim's head, probably made with a large rock, may actually have finished him off. He had been found around ten-thirty that Friday morning, and had been killed only a short time earlier.

Rummaging through his pockets, DI Protheroe found a wallet and provisionally identified him as Robert

Bell, 42. He lived some distance away, in a well-to-do area of Dinas Powys. Apart from Howard Jones' old Vauxhall, there was only one other car in the lay-by, a brand new BMW, which may have belonged to the deceased. DI Protheroe asked PC Watkins to phone the station to check, and he found that it did indeed belong to Robert Bell.

DI Protheroe spoke his thoughts out loud, "Bell was obviously murdered, as there's no possible cause of his injuries lying around nearby. Judging by the flattened grass from here towards the woods, the killer must have dragged the body here, presumably from near where the stick was found, apparently quite openly and publicly and at considerable risk to himself. But why drag him back to the lay-by and then leave him propped up here, again quite openly and publicly, so close to the road?"

He thought he was talking to himself, but PC Watkins was actually listening for once. PC Watkins was often to be found reading detective novels in his working hours (although it has to be said he mainly read the more lurid graphic novels, as he averred, he preferred "long pictures to long words"). He always said he was actually doing his police training. Now he realised was the time to show much he had learnt.

"Murderers often put their victims in prominent positions so that the bodies can be found quickly and provide a more accurate time of death, usually to fit in with the murderer's faked alibi."

DI Protheroe nodded. "Yes, Watkins. That's often the case." PC Watkins beamed with pride.

DI Protheroe asked Howard Jones to try and indicate roughly where Debbie had found the stick. But it was easily found anyway, as the grass was still showing the tracks made when the body had been dragged.

DI Protheroe left PC Watkins to take a short statement from Howard Jones and then had a look around.

When Watkins had finished, and the bored Debbie had been allowed to go home, DI Protheroe had a quick look on the online map display on his phone.

"You know there are very few houses around here, Watkins. Very few indeed. In fact, there only seems to be that one."

He pointed above the trees, where a small spiral of smoke was curling upwards from a hidden chimney.

"Perhaps the owner would have heard or seen something."

Carlton Grange was a large, but very rundown, detached house separated from the main road by a small unkempt garden. It had a 'For sale' sign outside.

DI Protheroe knocked on the door. After a few seconds, a small, wizened head appeared around the door. "I'm sorry, I only allow people to look over the house if they have an appointment with Milord."

DI Protheroe was a little taken aback by the requested involvement of a higher authority, until he remembered that Milord was the name of the estate agents on the board outside.

But David Marshall invited the detectives in as soon as he was shown identification. He said he had had the house on the market for some time, "It is rather in need of a little TLC," he admitted.

"A lot," thought DI Protheroe. But he wondered why Marshall had been so reluctant to allow potential visitors in without an appointment if he were having trouble selling the house.

In answer to DI Protheroe's queries, Marshall could only say "I've been in all day. I haven't even been outside these four walls. And I haven't seen anyone, not even the postman."

"Perhaps you've heard something unusual," ventured DI Protheroe.

Marshall shook his head.

"And did you know the deceased, Robert Bell?"

Marshall again shook his head.

As they left, PC Watkins muttered "So, a dead end."

DI Protheroe nodded. "Indeed, it would seem so."

Even Milord said they hadn't sent anybody around for weeks. Having seen the state of the house, DI Protheroe could understand why.

-oOo-

Natalya Bell lived in Dinas Powys, in a large, detached house that would have been described as a mansion anywhere else.

'Casa Campanil' looked huge from the outside, but DI Protheroe was taken aback at how much larger it seemed inside. It appeared that the whole of the ground floor had been designed as one huge living space. There was a fireplace that might very well have been transported there from an ancient castle, and a television that would not have disgraced a medium-sized cinema. Outside on the patio was a shower cubicle clearly for the use of those enjoying the swimming-pool, which DI Protheroe couldn't see but realised must be out there somewhere, probably ostentatiously hidden just out of view, as he could smell the chlorine.

Natalya appeared to have got over her grief by now as she seemed quite chirpy after an initial minute of looking downcast. DI Protheroe wondered whether that was because she had already checked what she was due to inherit.

"Yeah, well, Bobbie's done very well for himself, hasn't he? I mean, he only studied at some grotty secondary school in Penarth, and now he's the CEO and owner of several companies ... and he has a Rolex, a Beamer, this house ... and me!"

DI Protheroe winced, "And what exactly was his business?"

Natalya looked blank. "He brought home lots of money. I know all of it was legal, as Bobbie would never do anything criminal. But he made his money from ... well, from owning companies. He had lots of portfolios, you know."

Natalya didn't seem unintelligent, so perhaps her husband's work really was that vague. DI Protheroe decided it wouldn't be worth his while to ask her what the portfolios were.

"What about his colleagues and associates? Did Mr. Bell have any enemies?"

"Oh no. Well, yes. Er, I suppose he must have. I mean, he was so so successful in business, he must have trampled on a few toes, mustn't he? Some people might have felt upset that they had lost their money or their jobs, but that was their own fault, wasn't it? And people must have been jealous of his wealth and power and, shall we say, trappings." She seemed to indicate herself.

"And there were no problems of a personal nature? No other outside interests?"

Natalya shook her head so that her earrings rattled. "He had me and that was enough."

"And where did he go this morning?"

"He set off around eight in his Beamer. He loved that car. I suppose I shall have to sell it now as it's manual. Hey, I could get something in pink."

"This morning?" DI Protheroe prompted.

"Oh, he was going to some conference or a meeting or something at … do you know Harrison Holdings?"

DI Protheroe nodded. Leckwith Woods would have been on the route from Dinas Powys to Harrison Holdings' office in Cardiff.

"Well, he never got there," added Natalya unnecessarily.

-oOo-

DI Protheroe arranged to meet his brother, Merlin, in the 'Blue Anchor,' their favourite watering hole. He explained the current situation with the case.

Merlin mused, "I've been wondering why the killer dragged the body into such a prominent and noticeable location. If it were to roughly fix the time of death to support someone's faked alibi, then whose alibi are you supposed to be checking?"

"No, I'm sure the reason must have been that the killer was trying to move the focus of the crime away from where it actually took place."

"How old would you say David Marshall was?" asked Merlin, seeming to change the subject.

"About 42?" suggested DI Protheroe.

"That fits in with a possible theory," replied Merlin. "Which, with the question as to why the body was moved, gives me an idea … one that suggests just one suspect."

"I think we need to revisit the scene of the crime."

DI Protheroe nodded for no particular reason.

-oOo-

DI Protheroe, Merlin and PC Watkins arrived outside David Marshall's house.

Before knocking on the door, Merlin hunted around a little outside, where he found a large muddy patch. That was rather unusual as it had not rained for some time, so there was clearly a drainage problem here. There were also clear tyre marks in the mud. DI Protheroe asked PC Watkins to check these against the tyres on Robert Bell's BMW. There was also a shoe imprint.

DI Protheroe and his brother knocked on Marshall's front door.

This time, David Marshall looked upset that his visitors weren't coming to look over the house.

Marshall reiterated that he hadn't been outside the house all day and hadn't seen or heard anything suspicious.

But he seemed relatively happy to accede to DI Protheroe's request to view the house, although he must have realised it was more as an aspect of the investigation rather than a prospective viewing.

And there was a large clod of fresh mud in the front bedroom.

Marshall however refused to give his fingerprints. "Now that's going too far. That's an invasion of my privacy and rights." He seemed a little anxious though.

There was knock at the door.

This time, Marshall seemed to know that it was no prospective buyer.

PC Watkins stepped into the hall and asked to speak to his boss. Marshall hovered in the kitchen.

"The tyre prints seem a good match, Sir. One of the forensics lads was there too, and he agrees, although he was a little guarded in his opinion until he's done a thorough check."

DI Protheroe told Merlin that there was a match and then looked enquiringly at him for the next step.

Merlin pursed his lips. "So, there are only two explanations I can think of. Either Bell parked outside Marshall's house, then drove to the lay-by, walked back to the area behind the house, got himself murdered, and then got dragged back to the lay-by ... which, frankly, I find rather unlikely ... or ..."

"There's the point that Marshall claimed he hadn't left the house all day, and yet there was a fresh lump of mud in the bedroom. It hasn't rained for days and there was only that one patch of mud in front of the house ... which may be Marshall's, if he was lying ... or Bell's."

"I think we have enough information to at least take Mr. Marshall in for questioning. And we should be able to get his fingerprints and perhaps DNA."

-oOo-

David Marshall protested a lot at first, but soon became resigned to his fate. Especially after he had admitted he had been at St. Cyres Secondary School in the same year as Robert Bell.

And especially since his fingerprints were on the BMW and the murder weapon.

Bell had clearly been murdered spontaneously and the murder had not been planned … or certainly not well-planned.

-oOo-

Faced with the evidence, David Marshall confessed.

He seemed relieved to do so.

"The day had started off like any other day."

"Then there was a knock at the door, and there was Robert Bell."

"I didn't recognise him at first. He had changed a lot. When I was at school with him he was clean-shaven and overweight. Now he had what I suppose one would describe as designer stubble and he obviously worked out in a gym. And he was very expensively dressed."

"But he recognised me straight away. I suppose I haven't changed much over the years. Unlike him, I'm still overweight, and my clothes are more Skid Row than Savile Row."

"I don't know if he were just passing and saw the 'For Sale' sign, or whether he had seen me in the garden on a previous day and knew I lived there. He was clearly able to recognise me easily. As I said, I haven't changed much in decades."

"He asked if he could view the house. Well, I'm pretty desperate about selling the place and am perfectly happy to let anyone in, even without an appointment. It was my mother's house until she passed away two years ago. She hadn't looked after it for years, and I could ill afford to spend any money on it."

"I invited him in, already prepared to drop the price considerably. I rather hoped he was some property developer who had plans for the area."

"But I never found out what his business was. He just said how disgusting the house was and pointed out how little I had done with my life. OK, so I haven't been very lucky in my career choices since school, but he was so insufferably rude. I began to remember that he was just like that when we were in school. He was always bullying me."

"We went into the garden, and then into the large grassy area behind the house. I suppose I hoped that I might be able to suggest that the whole area was ripe for development."

"But then I became convinced that he had no interest in buying the property whatsoever, indeed perhaps he never had had any, and I had no idea why he had knocked on my door in the first place. Having poured scorn on my house and my life, he proceeded to show me how well off he was. He showed me his Rolex, told me how much his suit had cost, described his oh-so-much bigger and more opulent house, promised to show me his BMW …"

"Well, he turned away to point out how unkempt and hopelessly overgrown the garden was. I usually use a stout stick when I go into the garden, mainly to help me negotiate the steps there, and, well, I am afraid I hit him with the stick. It was just once, but I was so incensed that I must have been a lot more forceful than I had intended to be. Or maybe not."

"After I had hit him, I finished him off with a lump of concrete that was lying around. Then I dragged him away from my house, as there aren't many in the area. I'm not very fit, but it was important to get him away, so I dragged him all the way to that lay-by where you found him. I should have realised I could have taken him in his BMW, because I had to shift it afterwards anyway. He'd parked it outside my house, so I moved it to the lay-by near the body."

"To tell you the truth, I didn't know whether I was being very clever or very stupid. I just didn't really think at all."

"Actually, I don't really feel too bad about what I did. In fact, I think that perhaps I should have done it to him whilst we were at school. Then at least I would have felt I'd done something useful with my life."

-oOo-

"You know," said Merlin thoughtfully, "I often wonder how long it would take the police to find dead bodies if it weren't for early-morning dog walkers."

DI Protheroe shook his head. "There are always joggers," he said.

Case 2023/018

Up Before the Beak

Julie Whitehouse phoned up the police.

She seemed strangely giggly.

"Someone has just tried to rape me," she said a little breathlessly, before dissolving into a fit of giggles.

-oOo-

Detective Inspector Arthur Protheroe realised that the crime was of the utmost seriousness. As did his brother, Merlin, who had been inveigled into tagging along in an unofficial capacity.

But Julie would just not stop giggling.

"It was so funny," she said. "OK, so I have lots of bruises and a cut lip and I suppose a black eye, but it could have been so much worse."

"There was me in the garden, trying to sunbathe, when this lout … oh, I'd easily recognise him again, no problem … looked over the hedge, saw me, and then forced me into a, shall we say, unnatural position over the patio table."

"Just as he had got my, er, nether garments off, he screamed loudly, and then he ran shrieking out of the garden. He was desperately trying to pull his shorts up, and he even fell over once, into the fishpond. It was so funny."

"So, what stopped him from persisting in his attack?" asked DI Protheroe solicitously.

"Well, I could see blood streaming down his neck. And he was waving his arms about as if he were desperately trying to fight off some imaginary attacker. And then I saw Satan ..."

"Satan?" enquired Merlin, who had been rather quiet up until now.

"My cockatoo, of course," replied Julie. "Despite my plight, I don't think the devil would have intervened personally."

"My darling cockatoo had used her beak and claws and drawn blood from my would-be rapist's head."

"It was so funny!"

"So, where is the cockatoo now?" asked DI Protheroe.

Julie looked a little taken aback. "Oh, I don't know. Whilst I was recovering from the attack and phoning you, I forgot all about her."

DI Protheroe sent Merlin to have a look for the bird whilst he continued talking to Julie. She had not seemed to need comforting up until now, but now she began to worry about the cockatoo.

Merlin returned, looking a little downcast. "The lout must have found some sort of weapon. I'm afraid the cockatoo is no longer with us."

Julie seemed to take a lot longer to recover from this news than from the attack itself, but she eventually managed to provide a detailed and accurate description of her attacker.

DI Protheroe thought he recognised him straight away. Darren James was a local lad who seemed to feel it was his right to have his way with every young girl in the area. He had already been involved in a few serious, but not quite serious enough, incidents in the recent past.

An identity parade was arranged, and Julie picked him out easily.

But Darren James had an alibi, clearly concocted with his mates, but one a lawyer would find most helpful. And they were able to explain away the abrasions to his head.

DI Protheroe knew he needed something else as evidence.

And it was Merlin who came up with the solution.

The cockatoo's beak and claws were examined for DNA ... which provided a perfect match with that of Darren James.

This enabled DI Protheroe to request a more exhaustive and in-depth search of Julie Whitehouse's home. And traces of Darren James' blood were found on the patio table, placing him at the scene of the crime.

Julie Whitehouse was relieved to learn that her attacker was now 'doing bird.'

Case 2023/019

A True Gentleman?

"It seems you can't even trust a gentleman these days," said Jean Hartley sadly. "And he seemed such a nice old dear. I would never have thought he would have given me a false address."

Merlin Protheroe leant back in his office chair. He had been listening for some time to Mrs. Hartley bewailing the morals and integrity of the average "gentleman" these days, and he decided it was now time to try and get some details of why she had decided to call upon him professionally.

"So, you were returning from a week in a holiday cottage in Pembrokeshire and you had an accident, yes?"

"Well, no. *I* didn't have an accident. As the so-called gentleman admitted, it was all his fault. I was very impressed with the fact that he didn't argue or try to browbeat a lady driver but acknowledged that he had pulled out in front of me, and that I was not to blame to any degree."

"Perhaps you would describe exactly what happened … er, without any unnecessary digressions," suggested Merlin.

"Oh, I would never say anything that wasn't absolutely pertinent, I can assure you, Mr. Protheroe."

"Well, we had had a lovely week in Pembrokeshire, visiting the little seaside towns and their shops, and we saw dolphins and seals, and …"

Mrs. Hartley noticed that Merlin had raised one eyebrow, something he had been practising for a long time, purely to be able to achieve the right effect, in this case that of bringing Mrs. Hartley back down to earth with a bump.

"Well, I was driving back, travelling at a sensible speed, and this car pulled out from a side road right in front of me. The driver apologised and we exchanged addresses, and he showed me his insurance documents. I didn't have mine on me, but he seemed happy to accept that I was insured."

"Did you note down the details of his insurance policy?" asked Merlin.

"Oh, should I have done?" asked Mrs. Hartley. "There are always so many things to remember when you have an accident, aren't there? And it's such a long time since I had an accident with the car … er, it was August last year, I think."

"Anyway, he told me his address and I wrote it down in my notebook. It seemed such a nice place to live, Pembroke, you know."

"And I assume you have the car's registration number."

"Of course, do you think I'm a complete idiot?"

She reeled off the car's number without consulting the notebook she had laid on the desk in front of her.

Merlin frowned and then queried her ability to remember the number so easily.

"Oh, you mean *his* car number?"

"Well, I wrote it down on the next page of my notebook, but I must have used the back of it for a shopping list and I don't have it any more."

"Have you any idea what make of car it was?" asked Merlin, already anticipating the sort of response he was likely to receive.

"Well, it was white, and it was a Ford …"

"And the model? Focus, Fiesta, that sort of thing."

"… or a Vauxhall or a Wolseley, I suppose."

"So," said Merlin, resignedly, "It was white, and it was smaller than a Rolls-Royce or a Hispano Suiza?"

Mrs. Hartley nodded as if to suggest that that's all one really would be expected to remember.

"And the address he gave you?" asked Merlin, holding out his hand for the notebook and fully expecting to be told that Mrs. Hartley had used the page for something unmentionable.

"Here it is," said Mrs. Hartley, tearing out a small sheet of paper from the notebook. "But I checked, and so did my son, and it doesn't exist."

"I asked the gentleman where he lived, and he said Pembroke. I asked what the road was, and he replied Chapel View. He added the number 10B."

Merlin looked at the paper. It indeed read

10B Chapel View
Pembroke

"And you're sure that this is the address he gave you, this Mr., er, what was his name?"

"Llewellyn. I was surprised at first, as I thought he said Sue Ellen, like that woman in the Dallas TV series, but, no, it was definitely Llewellyn."

"And the surname?"

"Oh, he did tell me, but it was very Welsh and I couldn't get my head around it. I had his address anyway."

"But the address doesn't exist?"

"No, the crafty devil! And he told me very carefully what the address was for me to write it down. If he lived in number 10B, it was clearly a flat or an apartment, or maybe a penthouse."

Merlin had an idea, and suggested Mrs. Hartley left the matter with him for a day or so. He said he would get back to her ...

-oOo-

… which he soon did.

"I have some good news for you, Mrs. Hartley."

"The driver of the vehicle which collided with your car was Mr. Llewellyn Vaughan-Gwilliam, a well-respected solicitor from Pembrokeshire."

"Well, if he is so well-respected, why did the bounder give me a false address?" Mrs. Hartley said, indignantly.

"He didn't give you a false address, Mrs. Hartley."

"Of course he did. Do you think I'm an idiot?"

Merlin merely said, "He gave you a valid address, which you wrote down incorrectly. He lives in a house called 'Pembroke' in a road called Chapel View … in Tenby."

"Oh yes, we went to Tenby. It's a very nice place, although it did seem very full of people celebrating one thing and another. Maybe I shall call in on Mr. Vaughan-Gwilliam when I'm there next."

Mrs. Hartley said thank you, paid her bill, and wandered off a little distractedly.

Merlin thought he'd let her get well away from the area before he began his drive home.

Case 2023/020

Below Cheese Copse

Not a play for voices

To begin at the beginning:

After a few difficult cases, Private Investigator Merlin Protheroe decided he needed a holiday ... away from Penarth, crime, and even people.

So he chose a week in a holiday cottage in West Wales, in little Llanmad, although he checked first that the name didn't reflect the mental state of its inhabitants ...

-oOo-

As the ever-so-early sun weakly warms up the surrounding dew-dappled, cow-cudded, sheep-sauntering fields, Llanmad opens its bleary beer-distorted eyes to a rude and ruddy dawn. On Cheese Copse hanging Damocles-like above the town, wind-warped willows and browbeaten beeches tumble down the tumble-down holy hill to the cloistered church of St. Mad, named for the town's patron saint, a local girl, the fair lady Madeleine, known for her miracles and nominative brevity.

The Reverend Jenkin Elias looks from his lofty perch towards the town as it slowly awakens with little sense of urgency as Silly Willy the postman follows the fleet feet of the milkman as he weaves his wiggling way between the helter-skelter houses. Far out, the sun begins its task of warming the cockle-encrusted boat-bobbing sea, with no chance of its warmth ever reaching Llanmad itself. Salt-and-peppery sailors burnish brass and blistered bronze, and idle boys pretend to fish from the jetty, fully intending to return home just as the local chip shop opens.

On Abdication Street, Mrs. Porthcawl-Bevan opens her neat and natty guest-house, confusingly called The Original Number Twelve, as she insists it was before the Great Renumbering. She rarely accepts guests unless they are genteel gentlemen or proficient professionals, owing to her domestic spick-and-spannery. This week however she has graciously granted ingress to Merlin Protheroe, a policeman of sorts, hopefully a couth sleuth, from far-flung foreign lands in the English part of Wales.

Although his arrival was only the previous eight of the clock, the whole village is now fully aware and awarned of his residence amid salacious and scurrilous rumours of his possible motives.

What is that! A rat-a-tat on Mrs. Porthcawl-Bevan's rat-a-tattery door. She pokes her perfumed head out of the small but nearest-to-the-door window.

POLICE CONSTABLE GENGHIS REES

I have reason to speak with Merlin Protheroe,
Whose presence here is sought.
There is some matter that needs his wit.
There's a felon who must be caught.

MRS. PORTHCAWL-BEVAN

He's fast asleep. He's still in bed.
He got in really late.
I'd waken him, but he needs the rest,
So I'm afraid you'll have to wait.

POLICE CONSTABLE GENGHIS REES

I am the Law,
And my word is Law,
(*thoughtfully*) But he's a policeman of sorts,
So perhaps I can wait some more.

Having risen early and blearily, Merlin Protheroe overhears all this at the drop of an eave. Muttering mildly as his head encounters bare and bleakly unyielding rafters, he wonders whether the inhabitants of West Wales even curse in rhyme or at least in blank verse. He creakily negotiates the out-of-the-ark archaic wooden staircase to meet PC Rees at the door.

POLICE CONSTABLE GENGHIS REES

I am really sorry to bother you, Sir,
But if you would be so kind …
We have a problem and we'd like some help

from,
Shall we say, a rather less rustic mind.

As the watchful windows of the little town open and the twitchy net curtains are patted into place, Protheroe and Rees take slippery slidy steps down the careless ozone-spattered cobbles to the haven of the harbour, where the Topsy-Teifi River enters the sea reluctantly, losing its watery independence for the common good.

At the water's edge, police officials are froing and toing and desperately trying to hold back the eager scandalmongers of the village, as the grapevine has by now ensured that no-one could invent sufficient reason to remain at home.

A POLICE OFFICIAL

It's Tomas Nydahl, Genghis.
He must have hit his head.
He must have fallen down these concrete steps,
And now I'm sure he's dead.

Poor Tomas Nydahl was no famous tennis player, but just a peripatetic seafarer who had visited the little village and had fallen for it ... and down some concrete steps.

MERLIN PROTHEROE (*to everyone assembled there, at least officially*)

Good morning. Are there any more details of the, er, incident?

Poor Protheroe decides he won't even try to speak in blank verse. After all, he was almost from England.

MERLIN PROTHEROE (*looking around*)

Let's see. There are two pubs alongside each other here, both facing the sea. Isn't that rather a lot of pubs for a small village like this?

POLICE CONSTABLE GENGHIS REES

Do you really think two pubs a lot?
We all need our beer and grub.
But there are nine other pubs in our little town,
And we've one church for every pub.

'Twas in 'The Sailor's Arms'
That young Tomas always went.
Never more than ten pints he'd have,
And then he'd be homeward bent.

He'd leave the pub and teeter forth
Beside the Eastern Dock.
Then left he'd turn and stagger home,
And be back by twelve o'clock.

MERLIN PROTHEROE

OK, so there are two little docks, each with a few small boats moored, one in front of each pub. If he left 'The Sailor's Arms', the nearer pub to his house, then why did he fall down the steps in front of the, er, Western Dock, I suppose it's called. That's the dock in front of 'The Sailor's Legs' ... er, but isn't that a bit confusing? I mean, their having similar names ...

POLICE CONSTABLE GENGHIS REES

At one time sailors did not read much,
But I do see what you mean.
But it's not confusing to seafaring folk,
As one door's red and the other's green.

MERLIN PROTHEROE

So the question is, did he fall or was he pushed? The doctor says that the abrasions were consistent with a fall onto the concrete steps, around midnight. But I can understand why you wanted me to look into this, as you might want someone impartial and not connected with any of the local folk.

POLICE CONSTABLE GENGHIS REES

Actually, we were all rather worried that you might get
A trifle bored in our little town.
We all thought a possible murder might be the very thing
To stop you feeling down.

MERLIN PROTHEROE

Er, yes. I think we ought to visit 'The Sailor's Arms,' er, the one with the green door.

POLICE CONSTABLE GENGHIS REES

The landlord's Captain Seadog.
You'll find him rather deaf.
He can be a little bit rough as well.
He once lynched his short order chef.

The interior of 'The Sailor's Arms' is done up in a trendy pubchainery sort of way, although it has the naturally nautical look that only a fake modern pub renovation can achieve, and has been unaltered since before the War, the Boer War perhaps. Captain Seadog is seated behind his bar tapping out a rhythm on his seafaring fingers although no music is being played.

He clearly knows why he is receiving this visitation of officialdom.

CAPTAIN SEADOG

If you're asking about young Tomas,
He wasn't in last night.
He's usually in every evening,
So something isn't right.

But there's nothing more I can tell you,

Tho' I shall keep my ear to the ground.
If there's anyone spreading rumours,
Then I'll tell you what's going around.

It seemed nothing more could be gleaned from old seadog Seadog, so the two policemen leave the pub. Police Constable Genghis Rees avers that they probably won't hear anything from Captain Seadog anyway, as he's stone deaf and never hears a thing.

MERLIN PROTHEROE

Let's try the pub with the red door.

ROSIE PRICE

Welcome, welcome, one and all.
'The Sailor's Legs' will suit you nice.
Now do you want a pint or it is just a chat,
'Bout poor old Tomas, cold as ice?

We had a special party here
Last night, er, was it Friday?
And young Tomas, he was here,
All dressed up neat and tidy.

He left at twelve,
In a bit of a state.
But he knows his way home,
Right up to his gate.

And, before you ask,
He left on his own.

Nobody went back with him.
He was all alone.

Protheroe nods his head knowingly and noddingly. If he were to do this too often, he wonders if the locals would start calling him Noddy ... especially as he's just noticed that Police Constable Genghis Rees has exceptionally big ears.

MERLIN PROTHEROE

I think I know exactly what happened now. Because there was a party he wanted to go to, Tomas Nydahl went to 'The Sailor's Legs' last night, instead of his usual pub, 'The Sailor's Arms.' He left at twelve. But he was so used to walking home from his usual pub, and probably so drunk, that he thought he was walking along the side of the Eastern Dock, instead of alongside the Western Dock. He turned left as he usually would have done to reach his house ... and fell down the steps to his death.

POLICE CONSTABLE GENGHIS REES

Yes, I see now it must have been like that,
And it all falls into place.
We'll do a few checks and I think we'll find
That we can close the case.

So thank you for all your help.
You can now enjoy your time.
But I fear you'll be so utterly bored,
You'll crave another crime.

MERLIN PROTHEROE

That's no problem. I enjoyed the work.
It was a chance to use my brain.
So, just another few days,
And then I'm back by train.

Private Investigator Merlin Protheroe listened to himself and felt rather worried. Perhaps he'd been in Llanmad a little too long ...

By the same author

Inspector Pratt Goes Up to Eleven (published August 2023)

Paperback available on Amazon:
https://www.amazon.co.uk/dp/B0CDDNM1TM

Kindle available on Amazon:
https://www.amazon.co.uk/dp/B0CDCM3HWG

Inspector Pratt at Number Ten (published December 2022)

Paperback available on Amazon:
https://www.amazon.co.uk/dp/B0BQK6PMXW

Kindle available on Amazon:
https://www.amazon.co.uk/dp/B0BQJS4YTH

Inspector Pirat's Ninth (published October 2021)

Paperback available on Amazon:
https://www.amazon.co.uk/dp/B09HNRDQ1B

Kindle available on Amazon:
https://www.amazon.co.uk/dp/B09JN6GJ2R

Inspector Pirat's Pieces of Eight (published January 2021)

Paperback available on Amazon:
https://www.amazon.co.uk/dp/B08SLGF4HF

Kindle available on Amazon:
https://www.amazon.co.uk/dp/B08SLBGRKK

Inspector Pirat's Seventh Heaven (published May 2020)

Paperback available on Amazon:
https://www.amazon.co.uk/dp/1671837037

Kindle available on Amazon:
https://www.amazon.co.uk/dp/B088HHZY25

The Scrapbook of Inspector Pirat (published July 2019)

Paperback available on Amazon:
https://www.amazon.co.uk/dp/1099153611

Kindle available on Amazon:
https://www.amazon.co.uk/dp/B07STHZD8M

Inspector Pirat's Pick and Mix (published September 2018)

Paperback available on Amazon:
https://www.amazon.co.uk/dp/1724393782

Kindle available on Amazon:

https://www.amazon.co.uk/dp/B07HHG8LM5

The Rebirth of Inspector Pirat (published October 2017)

Paperback available on Amazon:
https://www.amazon.co.uk/dp/1974281523

Kindle available on Amazon:
https://www.amazon.co.uk/dp/B0765CJRN3

A Taste of Inspector Pirat (published July 2017)

A free sample of four previously-published Inspector Pirat stories

Kindle and PDF available free on Smashwords:
https://www.smashwords.com/books/view/734198

The Trial of Inspector Pirat (published February 2017)

Paperback available on Amazon:
https://www.amazon.co.uk/dp/1540693996

Kindle available on Amazon:
https://www.amazon.co.uk/dp/B06X6JLXMQ

Pirat's Early Cases (published April 2016)

Paperback available on Amazon:
https://www.amazon.co.uk/dp/1530449219

Kindle available on Amazon:
http://www.amazon.co.uk/dp/B01E7RP15A

The Return of Inspector Pirat: His First Book (published March 2015)

Paperback available on Amazon:
www.amazon.co.uk/dp/1511429461

Kindle available on Amazon:
www.amazon.co.uk/dp/B00UTKEKPM

Eric Bunnage wants to go down in history as one of the greatest ever … well, whatever. The only thing stopping him from achieving immortality is that he's just not very good at anything …

-

A Little Bit of Immortality (published February 2021)

Paperback available on Amazon:
https://www.amazon.co.uk/dp/B08WSC59LK

Kindle available on Amazon:
https://www.amazon.co.uk/dp/B08WPZPS9K

A history of Falconer and Watts, the long-established family coach company, which operated from Llanishen, Cardiff, from 1919 until 1982

<u>Memoirs of a Coach-Operating Man (published February 2018)</u>

Paperback available on Amazon:
<u>https://www.amazon.co.uk/dp/1985262738</u>

Kindle available on Amazon:

<u>https://www.amazon.co.uk/dp/B079VKWNYM</u>

A collection of short stories about the (fictional) pioneers of time travel

A Brief History of Time Travel (published January 2019)

Paperback available on Amazon:
https://www.amazon.co.uk/dp/179310204X

Kindle available on Amazon:
https://www.amazon.co.uk/dp/B07MQQCRWX

Another free book!

Because I found that so many of my friends were retiring and yet unprepared for so much leisure (and with so little money), I have written what I would describe as a small book or a large pamphlet, full of advice about retirement, entitled 'How to Retire Ungracefully.'

O.K., so it's not meant to be taken seriously, but, as I said, it's free, so you can check it out on Smashwords.

How to Retire Ungracefully (published April 2019)

Kindle and PDF available free on Smashwords:
https://www.smashwords.com/books/view/934785

And, for younger readers …

Joan Malone Alone (published August 2016)

Paperback available on Amazon:
https://www.amazon.co.uk/dp/1532972571

Kindle available on Amazon:
https://www.amazon.co.uk/dp/B01HSDJO30